Leveled Texts
for
Classic Fiction

Adventure

Collected and Leveled by Debra J. Housel

SHELL EDUCATION

Contributing Author

Wendy Conklin, M.S.

Publishing Credits

Dona Herweck Rice, *Editor-in-Chief*; Robin Erickson, *Production Director*;
Lee Aucoin, *Creative Director*; Timothy J. Bradley, *Illustration Manager*;
Sara Johnson, M.S.Ed., *Senior Editor*; Evelyn Garcia, *Associate Education Editor*;
Grace Alba, *Designer*; Corinne Burton, M.A.Ed., *Publisher*

Image Credits

Cover The Bridgeman Art Library, Shutterstock; p. 63, 65, 67, 69 Wikimedia; All other images Shutterstock

Standards
© 2004 Mid-continent Research for Education and Learning (McREL)
© 2010 National Governors Association Center for Best Practices and Council of Chief State School Officers (CCSS)

Shell Education

5301 Oceanus Drive
Huntington Beach, CA 92649

http://www.shelleducation.com

ISBN 978-1-4258-0983-6

© 2013 Shell Educational Publishing, Inc.

Table of Contents

What Is Fiction?

Fiction is the work of imaginative narration. In other words, it is something that is made, as opposed to something that has happened or something that is discovered. It helps bring our imaginations to life, since it offers an escape into a world where everything happens for a reason—nothing is by chance. Fiction includes three main elements: plot (sequence), character, and setting (place).

Each event occurs in a logical order, and somehow, the conflict is resolved. Fiction promises a resolution in the end, and so the reader waits for resolution as the characters change, grow, and survive experiences. We are drawn to fiction because it is very close to the story of our lives. Fiction suggests that our own stories will have meaning and a resolution in the end. Perhaps that might be the reason why we love fiction—it delivers what it promises.

Fiction compels its readers to care about the characters whether they are loyal friends or conniving enemies. Readers dream about the characters and mourn their heartaches. Readers might feel that they know a fictional character's story intimately because he or she reminds them of a friend or family member. Additionally, the place described in the story might feel like a real place the reader has visited or would like to visit.

Fiction vs. Nonfiction

Fiction is literature that stems from the imagination and includes genres such as mystery, adventure, fairy tales, and fantasy. Fiction can include facts, but the story is not true in its entirety. Facts are often exaggerated or manipulated to suit an author's intent for the story. Realistic fiction uses plausible characters and storylines, but the people do not really exist and/or the events narrated did not ever really take place. In addition, fiction is descriptive, elaborate, and designed to entertain. It allows readers to make their own interpretations based on the text.

Nonfiction includes a wide variety of writing styles that deal exclusively with real events, people, places, and things such as biographies, cookbooks, historical records, and scientific reports. Nonfiction is literature based on facts or perceived facts. In literature form, nonfiction deals with events that have actually taken place and relies on existing facts. Nonfiction writing is entirely fact-based. It states only enough to establish a fact or idea and is meant to be informative. Nonfiction is typically direct, clear, and simple in its message. Despite the differences, both fiction and nonfiction have a benefit and purpose for all readers.

The Importance of Using Fiction

Reading fiction has many benefits: It stimulates the imagination, promotes creative thinking, increases vocabulary, and improves writing skills. However, "students often hold negative attitudes about reading because of dull textbooks or being forced to read" (Bean 2000).

Fiction books can stimulate imagination. It is easy to get carried away with the character Percy Jackson as he battles the gods in *The Lightning Thief* (Riordan 2005). Readers can visualize what the author depicts. Researcher Keith Oatley (2009) states that fiction allows individuals to stimulate the minds of others in a sense of expanding on how characters might be feeling and what they might be thinking. When one reads fiction, one cannot help but visualize the nonexistent characters and places of the story. Lisa Zunshine (2006) has emphasized that fiction allows readers to engage in a theory-of-mind ability that helps them practice what the characters experience.

Since the work of fiction is indirect, it requires analysis if one is to get beyond the surface of the story. On the surface, one can view *Moby Dick* (Melville 1851) as an adventure story about a man hunting a whale. On closer examination and interpretation, the novel might be seen as a portrayal of good and evil. When a reader examines, interprets, and analyzes a work of fiction, he or she is promoting creative thinking. Creativity is a priceless commodity, as it facilitates problem solving, inventions, and creations of all kinds, and promotes personal satisfaction as well.

Reading fiction also helps readers build their vocabularies. Readers cannot help but learn a myriad of new words in Lemony Snicket's *A Series of Unfortunate Events* (1999). Word knowledge and reading comprehension go hand in hand. In fact, "vocabulary knowledge is one of the best predictors of reading achievement" (Richek 2005). Further, "vocabulary knowledge promotes reading fluency, boosts reading comprehension, improves academic achievement, and enhances thinking and communication" (Bromley 2004). Most researchers believe that students have the ability to add between 2,000 to 3,000 new words each school year, and by fifth grade, that number can be as high as 10,000 new words in their reading alone (Nagy and Anderson 1984). By exposing students to a variety of reading selections, educators can encourage students to promote the vocabulary growth that they need to be successful.

Finally, reading fictional text has a strong impact on students' ability as writers. According to Gay Su Pinnell (1988), "As children read and write, they make the connections that form their basic understandings about both….There is ample evidence to suggest that the processes are inseparable and that teachers should examine pedagogy in the light of these interrelationships." Many of the elements students encounter while reading fiction can transition into their writing abilities.

Text Complexity

Text complexity refers to reading and comprehending various texts with increasing complexity as students progress through school and within their reading development. The Common Core State Standards (2010) state that "by the time they [students] complete the core, students must be able to read and comprehend independently and proficiently the kinds of complex texts commonly found in college and careers." In other words, by the time students complete high school, they must be able to read and comprehend highly complex texts, so students must consistently increase the level of complexity tackled at each grade level. Text complexity relies on the following combination of quantitative and qualitative factors:

Quantitative Factors	
Word Frequency	This is how often a particular word appears in the text. If an unfamiliar high-frequency word appears in a text, chances are the student will have a difficult time understanding the meaning of the text.
Sentence Length	Long sentences and sentences with embedded clauses require a lot from a young reader.
Word Length	This is the number of syllables in a word. Longer words are not by definition hard to read, but certainly can be for young readers.
Text Length	This refers to the number of words within the text passage.
Text Cohesion	This is the overall structure of the text. A high-cohesion text guides readers by signaling relationships among sentences through repetition and concrete language. A low-cohesion text does not have such support.

The Importance of Using Fiction (cont.)

Qualitative Factors	
Level of Meaning or Purpose of Text	This refers to the objective and/or purpose for reading.
Structure	Texts that display low complexity are known for their simple structure. Texts that display high complexity are known for disruptions to predictable understandings.
Language Convention and Clarity	Texts that deviate from contemporary use of English tend to be more challenging to interpret.
Knowledge Demands	This refers to the background knowledge students are expected to have prior to reading a text. Texts that require students to possess a certain amount of previous knowledge are more complex than those that assume students have no prior knowledge.

(Adapted from the National Governors Association Center for Best Practices and Council of Chief State School Officers 2010)

The use of qualitative and quantitative measures to assess text complexity is demonstrated in the expectation that educators possess the ability to match the appropriate texts to the appropriate students. The passages in *Leveled Texts for Classic Fiction: Adventure* vary in text complexity and will provide leveled versions of classic complex texts so that educators can scaffold students' comprehension of these texts. Educators can choose passages for students to read based on the reading level as well as the qualitative and quantitative complexity factors in order to find texts that are "just right" instructionally.

Genres of Fiction

There are many different fiction genres. The *Leveled Texts for Classic Fiction* series focuses on the following genres: adventure, fantasy and science fiction, mystery, historical fiction, mythology, humor, and Shakespeare.

Adventure stories transport readers to exotic places like deserted islands, treacherous mountains, and the high seas. This genre is dominated by fast-paced action. The plot often focuses on a hero's quest and features a posse that helps him or her achieve the goal. The story confronts the protagonist with events that disrupt his or her normal life and puts the character in danger. The story involves exploring and conquering the unknown accompanied by much physical action, excitement, and risk. The experience changes the protagonist in many ways.

The Importance of Using Fiction *(cont.)*

Fantasy and science fiction are closely related. Fantasy, like adventure, involves quests or journeys that the hero must undertake. Within fantasy, magic and the supernatural are central and are used to suggest universal truths. Events happen outside the laws that govern our universe. Science fiction also operates outside of the laws of physics but typically takes place in the future, space, another world, or an alternate dimension. Technology plays a strong role in this genre. Both science fiction and fantasy open up possibilities (such as living in outer space and talking to animals) because the boundaries of the real world cannot confine the story. Ideas are often expressed using symbols.

Mystery contains intriguing characters with suspenseful plots and can often feel very realistic. The story revolves around a problem or puzzle to solve: *Who did it? What is it? How did it happen?* Something is unknown, or a crime needs to be solved. Authors give readers clues to the solution in a mystery, but they also distract the reader by intentionally misleading them.

Historical fiction focuses on a time period from the past with the intent of offering insight into what it was like to live during that time. This genre incorporates historical research into the stories to make them feel believable. However, much of the story is fictionalized, whether it is conversations or characters. Often, these stories reveal that concerns from the past are still concerns. Historical fiction centers on historical events, periods, or figures.

Myths are collections of sacred stories from ancient societies. Myths are ways to explain questions about the creation of the world, the gods, and human life. For example, mythological stories often explain why natural events like storms or floods occur or how the world and living things came to be in existence. Myths can be filled with adventures conflict, between humans, and gods with extraordinary powers. These gods possess emotions and personality traits that are similar to humans.

Humor can include parody, joke books, spoofs, and twisted tales, among others. Humorous stories are written with the intent of being light-hearted and fun in order to make people laugh and to entertain. Often, these stories are written with satire and dry wit. Humorous stories also can have a very serious or dark side, but the ways in which the characters react and handle the situations make them humorous.

Shakespeare's plays can be classified in three genres: comedy, tragedy, and history. Shakespeare wrote his plays during the late 1500s and early 1600s, and performed many of them in the famous Globe Theater in London, England. Within each play is not just one coherent story but also a set of two or three stories that can be described as "plays within a play." His plays offer multiple perspectives and contradictions to make the stories rich and interesting. Shakespeare is noted for his ability to bring thoughts to life. He used his imagination to adapt stories, history, and other plays to entertain his audiences.

Elements of Fiction

The many common characteristics found throughout fiction are known as the elements of fiction. Among such elements are *point of view*, *character*, *setting*, and *plot*. *Leveled Texts for Classic Fiction* concentrates on setting, plot, and character, with an emphasis on language usage.

Language usage typically refers to the rules for making language. This series includes the following elements: *personification*, *hyperbole*, *alliteration*, *onomatopoeia*, *imagery*, *symbolism*, *metaphor*, and *word choice*. The table below provides a brief description of each.

Language Usage	Definition	Example
Personification	Giving human traits to nonhuman things	The chair moaned when she sat down on it.
Hyperbole	Extreme exaggeration	He was so hungry, he could eat a horse.
Alliteration	Repetition of the beginning consonant sounds	She sold seashells by the seashore.
Onomatopoeia	Forming a word from the sound it makes	Knock-knock, woof, bang, sizzle, hiss
Imagery	Language that creates a meaningful visual experience for the reader	His socks filled the room with a smell similar to a wet dog on a hot day.
Symbolism	Using objects to represent something else	A heart represents *love*.
Metaphor	Comparison of two unrelated things	My father is the rock of our family.
Word Choice	Words that an author uses to make the story memorable and to capture the reader's attention	In chapter two of *Holes* by Louis Sachar (2000), the author directly addresses the reader, saying, "The reader is probably asking…." The author predicts what the reader is wondering.

Elements of Fiction (cont.)

Setting is the *where* and *when* of a story's action. Understanding setting is important to the interpretation of the story. The setting takes readers to other times and places. Setting plays a large part in what makes a story enjoyable for the reader.

Plot forms the core of what the story is about and establishes the chain of events that unfolds in the story. Plot contains a character's motivation and the subsequent cause and effect of the character's actions. A plot diagram is an organizational tool that focuses on mapping out the events in a story. By mapping out the plot structure, students are able to visualize the key features of a story. The following is an example of a plot diagram:

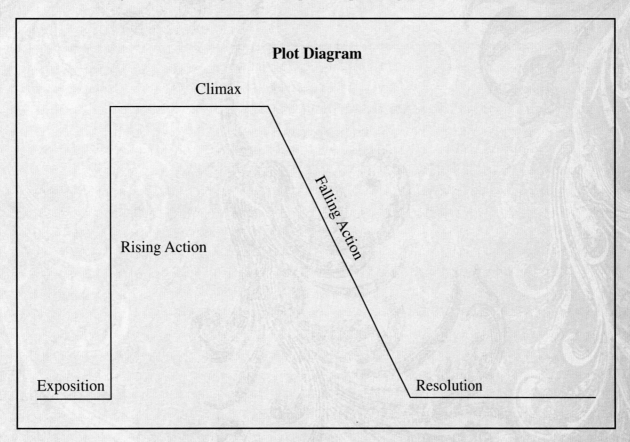

Characters are the people in the story. The protagonist is the main or leading character. He or she might be the narrator of the story. The antagonist is the force or character that acts against the protagonist. This antagonist is not always a person; it could be things such as weather, technology, or even a vehicle. Both the protagonist and antagonist can be considered dynamic, which means that they change or grow during the story as opposed to remaining static, or unchanging, characters. Readers engage with the text as they try to understand what motivates the characters to think and act as they do. Desires, values, and outside pressures all motivate characters' actions and help to determine the story's outcome.

A Closer Look at Adventure

Adventure stories typically include a courageous hero or heroine who attempts to solve all the problems with the assistance of a sidekick. This hero or heroine has a flaw that causes him or her trouble. The character makes a journey to solve a problem. The problem might be that someone is missing or a question might need answering. The character encounters conflict with nature, with self, and/or with another character. The ending might not be realistic, but in the end, the problem is solved and the main character may have transformed.

In this book, you will find stories from works of adventure from classic fiction. The titles are as follows:

- *Robinson Crusoe* by Daniel Defoe
- *Hans Brinker* by Mary Mapes Dodge
- *The Adventures of Tom Sawyer* by Mark Twain
- *The Swiss Family Robinson* by Johann Wyss
- *The Adventures of Huckleberry Finn* by Mark Twain
- *The Railway Children* by E. Nesbit
- *Rebecca of Sunnybrook Farm* by Kate Douglas Wiggin
- *Treasure Island* by Robert Louis Stevenson
- *Tarzan of the Apes* by Edgar Rice Burroughs
- *The Count of Monte Cristo* by Alexandre Dumas
- *The Merry Adventures of Robin Hood* by Howard Pyle
- *The Jungle Book* by Rudyard Kipling
- *What Katy Did* by Susan Coolidge
- *Call of the Wild* by Jack London
- *Kidnapped* by Robert Louis Stevenson

A Closer Look at Adventure (cont.)

Although there are many elements of fiction that can be studied in each passage of this book, the chart below outlines the strongest element portrayed in each passage.

Element of Fiction	Passage Title
Setting	• Excerpt from *Robinson Crusoe* • Excerpt from *Hans Brinker* • Excerpt from *The Adventures of Tom Sawyer*
Character	• Excerpt from *The Swiss Family Robinson* • Excerpt from *The Adventures of Huckleberry Finn* • Excerpt from *The Railway Children* • Excerpt from *Rebecca of Sunnybrook Farm*
Plot	• Excerpt from *Treasure Island* • Excerpt from *Tarzan of the Apes* • Excerpt from *The Count of Monte Cristo* • Excerpt from *The Merry Adventures of Robin Hood*
Language Usage	• Excerpt from *The Jungle Book* • Excerpt from *What Katy Did* • Excerpt from *Call of the Wild* • Excerpt from *Kidnapped*

Leveled Texts to Differentiate Instruction

Today's classrooms contain diverse pools of learners. Above-level, on-level, below-level, and English language learners all come together to learn from one teacher in one classroom. The teacher is expected to meet their diverse needs. These students have different learning styles, come from different cultures, experience a variety of emotions, and have varied interests. And, they differ in academic readiness when it comes to reading. At times, the challenges teachers face can be overwhelming as they struggle to create learning environments that address the differences in their students while at the same time ensure that all students master the required grade-level objectives.

What is differentiation? Tomlinson and Imbau say, "Differentiation is simply a teacher attending to the learning needs of a particular student or small group of students, rather than teaching a class as though all individuals in it were basically alike" (2010). Any teacher who keeps learners at the forefront of his or her instruction can successfully provide differentiation. The effective teacher asks, "What am I going to do to shape instruction to meet the needs of all my learners?" One method or methodology will not reach all students.

Differentiation includes what is taught, how it is taught, and the products students create to show what they have learned. When differentiating curriculum, teachers become organizers of learning opportunities within the classroom environment. These opportunities are often referred to as *content*, *process*, and *product*.

- **Content:** Differentiating the content means to put more depth into the curriculum through organizing the curriculum concepts and structure of knowledge.

- **Process:** Differentiating the process requires using varied instructional techniques and materials to enhance student learning.

- **Product:** Cognitive development and students' abilities to express themselves improves when products are differentiated.

Leveled Texts to Differentiate Instruction (cont.)

Teachers should differentiate by content, process, and product according to students' differences. These differences include student *readiness*, *learning styles*, and *interests*.

- **Readiness:** If a learning experience aligns closely with students' previous skills and understanding of a topic, they will learn better.

- **Learning styles:** Teachers should create assignments that allow students to complete work according to their personal preferences and styles.

- **Interests:** If a topic sparks excitement in the learners, then students will become involved in learning and better remember what is taught.

Typically, reading teachers select different novels or texts that are leveled for their classrooms because only one book may either be too difficult or too easy for a particular group of students. One group of students will read one novel while another group reads another, and so on. What makes *Leveled Texts for Classic Fiction: Adventure* unique is that all students, regardless of reading level, can read the same selection from a story and can participate in whole-class discussions about it. This is possible because each selection is leveled at four different reading levels to accommodate students' reading abilities. Regardless of the reading level, all of the selections present the same content. Teachers can then focus on the same content standard or objective for the whole class, but individual students can access the content at their particular instructional levels rather than their frustration level and avoid the frustration of a selection at too high or low a level.

ELL Level

Below Level

On Level

Above Level

Leveled Texts to Differentiate Instruction (cont.)

Teachers should use the texts in this series to scaffold the content for their students. At the beginning of the year, students at the lowest reading levels may need focused teacher guidance. As the year progresses, teachers can begin giving students multiple levels of the same text to allow them to work independently at improving their comprehension. This means that each student will have a copy of the text at his or her independent reading level and at the instructional reading level. As students read the instructional-level texts, they can use the lower-leveled texts to better understand difficult vocabulary. By scaffolding the content in this way, teachers can support students as they move up through the reading levels and encourage them to work with texts that are closer to the grade level at which they will be tested.

A teacher does not need to draw attention to the fact that the texts are leveled. Nor should they hide it. Teachers who want students to read the text together can use homogeneous groups and distribute the texts after students join the groups. Or, teachers can distribute copies of the appropriate level to each student by copying the pages and separating them by each level.

Teaching Suggestions

Strategies for Higher-Order Thinking

Open-ended questions are a great way to infuse higher-order thinking skills into instruction. Open-ended questions have many appropriate answers and are exclusively dependent on the creativity of the student. Rarely do these questions have only one correct answer. It is up to the students to think and decide on their own what the answer should be. This is critical thinking at its very best. The following are some characteristics of open-ended questions:

> - They ask students to *think* and *reflect*.
> - They ask students to provide their *feelings* and *opinions*.
> - They make students responsible for the *control* of the conversation.

There are many reasons to prefer open-ended over closed-ended questions. First, students must know the facts of the story to answer open-ended questions. Any higher-order question by necessity will encompass lower-order, fact-based questions. For a student to be able to answer a *what if* question (which is an example of an open-ended question), he or she must know the content of the story (which is a lower-level fact).

Open-ended questions also stimulate students to go beyond typical questions about a text. They spark real conversations about a text and are enriching. As a result, more students will be eager to participate in class discussions. In a more dynamic atmosphere, students will naturally make outside connections to the text, and there will be no need to force such connections.

Some students may at first be resistant to open-ended questions because they are afraid to think creatively. Years of looking for the one correct answer may make many students fear failure and embarrassment if they get the "wrong" answer. It will take time for these students to feel at ease with these questions. Model how to answer such questions. Keep encouraging students to answer them. Most importantly, be patient. The following are some examples of open-ended questions:

- Why do you think the author selected this setting?

> - What are some explanations for the character's decisions?
> - What are some lessons that this passage can teach us?
> - How do the words set the mood or tone of this passage?

Teaching Suggestions (cont.)

Strategies for Higher-Order Thinking (cont.)

The tables below and on the following page are examples of open-ended questions and question stems that are specific to the elements of fiction covered in this series. Choose questions to challenge students to think more deeply about specific elements.

Setting
• In what ways did the setting…
• Describe the ways in which the author used setting to…
• What if the setting changed to…
• What are some possible explanations for selecting this setting?
• What would be a better setting for this story, and why is it better?
• Why did the author select this setting?
• What new element would you add to this setting to make it better?
• Explain several reasons why the characters fit well in this setting.
• Explain several reasons why the characters might fit better in a new setting.
• What makes this setting predictable or unpredictable?
• What setting would make the story more exciting? Explain.
• What setting would make the story dull? Explain.
• Why is the setting important to the story?

Character
• What is the likelihood that the character will…
• Form a hypothesis about what might happen to the character if…
• In what ways did the character show his/her thoughts by his/her actions?
• How might you have done this differently than the character?
• What are some possible explanations for the character's decisions about…
• Explain several reasons why the characters fit well in this setting.
• Explain several reasons why the characters don't fit well in this setting.
• What are some ways you would improve this character's description?
• Predict what the character will do next. Explain.
• What makes this character believable?
• For what reasons do you like or dislike this character?
• What makes this character memorable?
• What is the character thinking?

Teaching Suggestions (cont.)

Strategies for Higher-Order Thinking (cont.)

Plot

- How does this event affect…
- Predict the outcome…
- What other outcomes could have been possible, and why?
- What problems does this create?
- What is the likelihood…
- Propose a solution.
- Form a hypothesis.
- What is the theme of this story?
- What is the moral of this story?
- What lessons could this story teach us?
- How is this story similar to other stories you have read?
- How is this story similar to other movies you have watched?
- What sequel could result from this story?

Language Usage

- Describe the ways in which the author used language to…
- In what ways did language usage…
- What is the best description of…
- How would you have described this differently?
- What is a better way of describing this, and what makes it better?
- How can you improve upon the word selection…
- How can you improve upon the description of…
- What other words could be substituted for…
- What pictures do the words paint in your mind?
- How do the words set the mood or tone?
- Why would the author decide to use…
- What are some comparisons you could add to…
- In what ways could you add exaggeration to this sentence?

Teaching Suggestions *(cont.)*

Reading Strategies for Literature

The college and career readiness anchor standards within the Common Core State Standards in reading (National Governors Association Center for Best Practices and Council of Chief State School Officers 2010) include understanding key ideas and details, recognizing craft and structure, and being able to integrate knowledge and ideas. The following two pages offer practical strategies for achieving these standards using the texts found in this book.

Identifying Key Ideas and Details

- Have students work together to create talking tableaux based on parts of the text that infer information. A tableau is a freeze-frame where students are asked to pose and explain the scene from the text they are depicting. As students stand still, they take turns breaking away from the tableau to tell what is being inferred at that moment and how they know this. While this strategy is good for all students, it is a strong activity for **English language learners** because they have an opportunity for encoding and decoding with language and actions.

- Theme is the lesson that the story teaches its readers. It can be applied to everyone, not just the characters in the story. Have students identify the theme and write about what happens that results in their conclusions. Ask students to make connections as to how they can apply the theme to their lives. Allow **below-grade-level** writers to record this information, use graphic organizers for structure, or illustrate their answers in order to make the information more concrete for them.

- Have students draw a picture of the character during an important scene in the story, and use thought bubbles to show the character's secret thoughts based on specific details found in the text. This activity can benefit everyone, but it is very effective for **below-grade-level** writers and **English language learners**. Offering students an opportunity to draw their answers provides them with a creative method to communicate their ideas.

- Have students create before-and-after pictures that show how the characters change over the course of the story. Encourage **above-grade-level** students to examine characters' personality traits and how the characters' thoughts change. This activity encourages students to think about the rationale behind the personality traits they assigned to each character.

Teaching Suggestions (cont.)

Reading Strategies for Literature (cont.)

Understanding Craft and Structure

- Ask students to identify academic vocabulary in the texts and to practice using the words in a meet-and-greet activity in the classroom, walking around and having conversations using them. This gives **English language learners** an opportunity to practice language acquisition in an authentic way.

- Have students create mini-posters that display the figurative language used in the story. This strategy encourages **below-grade-level** students to show what they have learned.

- Allow students to work in pairs to draw sets of stairs on large paper, and then write how each part of the story builds on the previous part and fits together to provide the overall structure of the story. Homogeneously partner students so that **above-grade-level** students will challenge one another.

- Select at least two or three texts, and have students compare the point of view from which the different stories are narrated. Then, have students change the point of view (e.g., if the story is written in first person, have students rewrite a paragraph in third person). This is a challenging activity specifically suited for **on-grade-level** and **above-grade-level** students to stimulate higher-order thinking.

- Pose the following questions to students: What if the story is told from a different point of view? How does that change the story? Have students select another character's point of view and brainstorm lists of possible changes. This higher-order thinking activity is open-ended and effective for **on-level**, **above-level**, **below-level**, and **English language learners**.

Integrating Knowledge and Ideas

- Show students a section from a movie, a play, or a reader's theater about the story. Have students use graphic organizers to compare and contrast parts of the text with scenes from one of these other sources. Such visual displays support comprehension for **below-level** and **English language learners**.

- Have students locate several illustrations in the text, and then rate the illustrations based on their effective visuals. This higher-order thinking activity is open-ended and is great for **on-level**, **below-level**, **above-level**, and **English language learners**.

- Let students create playlists of at least five songs to go with the mood and tone of the story. Then instruct students to give an explanation for each chosen song. Musically inclined students tend to do very well with this type of activity. It also gives a reason for writing, which can engage **below-grade-level** writers.

- Have students partner up to create talk show segments that discuss similar themes found in the story. Each segment should last between one and two minutes and can be performed live or taped. Encourage students to use visuals, props, and other tools to make it real. Be sure to homogeneously group students for this activity and aid your **below-level** students so they can be successful. This activity allows for **all students** to bring their creative ideas to the table and positively contribute to the end result.

Teaching Suggestions *(cont.)*

Fiction as a Model for Writing

It is only natural that reading and writing go hand in hand in students' literacy development. Both are important for functioning in the real world as adults. Established pieces of fiction, like the ones in this book, serve as models for how to write effectively. After students read the texts in this book, take time for writing instruction. Below are some ideas for writing mini-lessons that can be taught using the texts from this book as writing exemplars.

How to Begin Writing a Story

Instead of beginning a story with '*Once upon a time*' or '*Long, long ago*,' teach students to mimic the styles of well-known authors. As students begin writing projects, show them a variety of first sentences or paragraphs written by different authors. Discuss how these selections are unique. Encourage students to change or adapt the types of beginnings found in the models to make their own story hooks.

Using Good Word Choice

Good word choice can make a significant difference in writing. Help students paint vivid word pictures by showing them examples within the passages found in this book. Instead of writing *I live in a beautiful house*, students can write *I live in a yellow-framed house with black shutters and white pillars that support the wraparound porch*. Encourage students to understand that writing is enriched with sensory descriptions that include what the characters smell, hear, taste, touch, and see. Make students aware of setting the emotional tone in their stories. For example, *In an instant, the hair on the back of his neck stood up, the door creaked open, and a hand reached through*. This example sets a scary mood. Hyperbole is also a great tool to use for effect in stories.

Character Names Can Have Meaning

Students can use names to indicate clues about their characters' personalities. Mrs. Strict could be a teacher, Dr. Molar could be a dentist, and Butch could be the class bully. Remind students that the dialogue between their characters should be real, not forced. Students should think about how people really talk and write dialogue using jargon and colorful words, for example, *"Hey you little twerp, come back here!" yelled Brutus.*

How to Use This Book

Classroom Management for Leveled Texts

Determining your students' instructional reading levels is the first step in the process of effectively managing the leveled-text passages. It is important to assess their reading abilities often so they do not get stuck on one level. Below are suggested ways to use this resource, as well as other resources available to you, to determine students' reading levels.

Running records: While your class is doing independent work, pull your below-grade-level students aside one at a time. Have them individually read aloud the lowest level of a text (the star level) as you record any errors they make on your own copy of the text. Assess their accuracy and fluency, mark the words they say incorrectly, and listen for fluent reading. Use your judgment to determine whether students seem frustrated as they read. If students read accurately and fluently and comprehend the material, move them up to the next level and repeat the process. Following the reading, ask comprehension questions to assess their understanding of the material. As a general guideline, students reading below 90 percent accuracy are likely to feel frustrated as they read. A variety of other published reading assessment tools are available to assess students' reading levels with the running-records format.

Refer to other resources: Another way to determine instructional reading levels is to check your students' Individualized Education Plans; ask the school's language development specialists and/or special education teachers; or review test scores. All of these resources can provide the additional information needed to determine students' reading levels.

How to Use This Book *(cont.)*

Distributing the Texts

Some teachers wonder about how to distribute the different-leveled texts within the classroom. They worry that students will feel insulted or insecure if they do not get the same material as their neighbors. Prior to distributing the texts, make sure that the classroom environment is one in which all students learn at their individual instructional levels. It is important to make this clear. Otherwise, students may constantly ask why their work is different from another student's work. Simply state that students will not be working on the same assignment every day and that their work may slightly vary to resolve students' curiosity. In this approach, distribution of the texts can be very open and causal, just like passing out any other assignment.

Teachers who would rather not have students aware of the differences in the texts can try the suggestions below:

- Make a pile in your hands from star to triangle. Put your finger between the circle and square levels. As you approach each student, pull from the top (star), above your finger (circle), below your finger (square), or the bottom (triangle), depending on each student's level. If you do not hesitate too much in front of each desk, students will probably not notice.

- Begin the class period with an opening activity. Put the texts in different places around the room. As students work quietly, circulate and direct students to the right locations for retrieving the texts you want them to use.

- Organize the texts in small piles by seating arrangement so that when you arrive at a group of desks, you will have only the levels you need.

How to Use This Book *(cont.)*

Components of the Product

Each passage is derived from classic literary selections. Classics expose readers to cultural heritage or the literature of a culture. Classics improve understanding of the past and, in turn, understanding of the present. These selections from the past explain how we got to where we are today.

The Levels

There are 15 passages in this book, each from a different work of classic fiction. Each passage is leveled to four different reading levels. The images and fonts used for each level within a work of fiction look the same.

Behind each page number, you will see a shape. These shapes indicate the reading levels of each piece so that you can make sure students are working with the correct texts. The chart on the following page provides specific levels of each text.

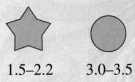

1.5–2.2   3.0–3.5

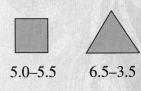

5.0–5.5   6.5–3.5

Leveling Process

The texts in this series are excerpts from classic pieces of literature. A reading specialist has reviewed each excerpt and leveled each one to create four distinct reading passages with unique levels.

Elements of Fiction Question

Each text includes one comprehension question that directs the students to think about the chosen element of fiction for that passage. These questions are written at the appropriate reading level to allow all students to successfully participate in a whole-class discussion. These questions are open-ended and designed to stimulate higher-order thinking.

Digital Resource CD

The Digital Resource CD allows for easy access to all the reading passages in this book. Electronic PDF files as well as word files are included on the CD.

How to Use This Book (cont.)

Title	ELL Level	Below Level	On level	Above level
Setting Passages	⭐ 1.5–2.2	⬤ 3.0–3.5	◼ 5.0–5.5	▲ 6.5–7.2
Robinson Crusoe	2.0	3.5	5.4	7.2*
Hans Brinker	2.1	3.4	5.0	7.1*
The Adventures of Tom Sawyer	2.1	3.4	5.1*	6.5
Character Passages				
The Swiss Family Robinson	2.1	3.3	5.3	6.5*
The Adventures of Huckleberry Finn	1.8	3.0	5.3*	6.5
The Railway Children	2.2	3.5*	5.0	6.5
Rebecca of Sunnybrook Farm	2.2	3.5	5.4*	6.5
Plot Passages				
Treasure Island	2.0	3.3	5.0*	7.0
Tarzan of the Apes	2.2	3.5	5.1	6.5*
The Count of Monte Cristo	1.5	3.2	5.0	6.9*
The Merry Adventures of Robin Hood	2.2	3.5	5.0	7.0*
Language Usage Passages				
The Jungle Book	2.0	3.5	5.5	6.5*
What Katy Did	2.1	3.4*	5.0	7.0
Call of the Wild	2.2	3.5	5.1	7.0*
Kidnapped	2.2	3.2	5.0	6.7*

* The passages with an asterisk indicate the reading passage from the original work of fiction.

Correlations to Standards

Shell Education is committed to producing educational materials that are research and standards based. In this effort, we have correlated all our products to the academic standards of all 50 United States, the District of Columbia, the Department of Defense Dependent Schools, and all Canadian provinces.

How to Find Standards Correlations

To print a customized correlations report of this product for your state, visit our website at **http://www.shelleducation.com** and follow the on-screen directions. If you require assistance in printing correlations reports, please contact Customer Service at 1-800-858-7339.

Purpose and Intent of Standards

Legislation mandates that all states adopt academic standards that identify the skills students will learn in kindergarten through grade twelve. Many states also have standards for pre-K. This same legislation sets requirements to ensure the standards are detailed and comprehensive.

Standards are designed to focus instruction and guide adoption of curricula. Standards are statements that describe the criteria necessary for students to meet specific academic goals. They define the knowledge, skills, and content students should acquire at each level. Standards are also used to develop standardized tests to evaluate students' academic progress.

Teachers are required to demonstrate how their lessons meet state standards. State standards are used in the development of all our products, so educators can be assured they meet the academic requirements of each state.

McREL Compendium

We use the Mid-continent Research for Education and Learning (McREL) Compendium to create standards correlations. Each year, McREL analyzes state standards and revises the compendium. By following this procedure, McREL is able to produce a general compilation of national standards. Each lesson in this product is based on one or more McREL standards. The chart on the following pages lists each standard taught in this product and the page numbers for the corresponding lessons.

TESOL Standards

The lessons in this book promote English language development for English language learners. The standards listed on the following pages support the language objectives presented throughout the lessons.

Common Core State Standards

The texts in this book are aligned to the Common Core State Standards (CCSS). The standards correlation can be found on pages 28–29.

Correlations to Standards *(cont.)*

Correlation to Common Core State Standards

The passages in this book are aligned to the Common Core State Standards (CCSS). Students who meet these standards develop the skills in reading that are the foundation for any creative and purposeful expression in language.

Grade(s)	Standard
3	RL.3.10—By the end of year, independently and proficiently read and comprehend literature, including stories, dramas, and poetry, at the high end of the grades 2–3 text-complexity band
4–5	RL.4.10–5.10—By the end of the year, proficiently read and comprehend literature, including stories, dramas, and poetry, in the grades 4–5 text-complexity band, with scaffolding as needed at the high end of the range
6–8	RL.6.10–8.10—By the end of the year, proficiently read and comprehend literature, including stories, dramas, and poems, in the grades 6–8 text-complexity band, with scaffolding as needed at the high end of the range.

As outlined by the Common Core State Standards, teachers are "free to provide students with whatever tools and knowledge their professional judgment and experience identify as most helpful for meeting the goals set out in the standards." Bearing this in mind, teachers are encouraged to use the recommendations indicated in the chart below in order to meet additional CCSS Reading Standards that require further instruction.

Standard	Additional Instruction
RL.3.1–5.1— Key Ideas and Details	• Ask and answer questions to demonstrate understanding of a text. • Refer to details and examples in a text. • Quote accurately from a text when explaining what the text says.
RL.3.2–5.2— Key Ideas and Details	• Recount stories to determine the central message, lesson, or moral and explain how it is conveyed. • Determine a theme of a story from details in the text.
RL.3.3–5.3— Key Ideas and Details	• Describe in depth a character, setting, or event in a story.
RL.6.1–8.1— Key Ideas and Details	• Cite textual evidence to support analysis of what the text says.
RL.6.2–8.2— Key Ideas and Details	• Determine a theme or central idea of a text and analyze its development over the course of the text.
RL.6.3–8.3— Key Ideas and Details	• Analyze how particular elements of a story or drama interact.

Correlations to Standards *(cont.)*

Correlation to Common Core State Standards *(cont.)*

Standard	Additional Instruction *(cont.)*
RL.3.4–8.4— Craft and Structure	• Determine the meaning of words and phrases as they are used in the text.
RL.3.5–5.5— Craft and Structure	• Refer to parts of stories when writing or speaking about a text. • Explain the overall structure of a story.
RL.3.6–8.6— Craft and Structure	• Distinguish and describe point of view within the story.
RL.6.5–8.5— Craft and Structure	• Analyze and compare and contrast the overall structure of a story.
RL.3.7–5.7— Integration of Knowledge and Ideas	• Explain how specific aspects of a text's illustrations contribute to what is conveyed by the words in a story.
RL.3.9–8.9— Integration of Knowledge and Ideas	• Compare and contrast the themes, settings, and plots of stories.

Correlation to McREL Standards

Standard	Page(s)
5.1—Previews text (3–5)	all
5.1—Establishes and adjusts purposes for reading (6–8)	all
5.2—Establishes and adjusts purposes for reading (3–5)	all
5.3—Makes, confirms, and revises simple predictions about what will be found in a text (3–5)	all
5.3—Uses a variety of strategies to extend reading vocabulary (6–8)	all
5.4—Uses specific strategies to clear up confusing parts of a text (6–8)	all
5.5—Use a variety of context clues to decode unknown words (3–5)	all
5.5—Understands specific devices an author uses to accomplish his or her purpose (6–8)	all
5.6—Reflects on what has been learned after reading and formulates ideas, opinions, and personal responses to texts (6–8)	all

Correlation to Standards (cont.)

Correlation to McREL Standards (cont.)

Standard	Page(s)
5.7—Understands level-appropriate reading vocabulary (3–5)	all
5.8—Monitors own reading strategies and makes modifications as needed (3–5)	all
5.10—Understands the author's purpose or point of view (3–5)	all
6.1—Reads a variety of literary passages and texts (3–5, 6–8)	all
6.2—Knows the defining characteristics and structural elements of a variety of literary genres (3–5, 6–8)	all
6.3—Understands the basic concept of plot (3–5)	all
6.3—Understands complex elements of plot development (6–8)	all
6.4—Understands similarities and differences within and among literary works from various genres and cultures (3–5)	all
6.4—Understands elements of character development (6–8)	all
6.5—Understands elements of character development in literary works (3–5)	all
6.7—Understands the ways in which language is used in literary texts (3–5)	all

Correlation to TESOL Standards

Standard	Page(s)
2.1—Students will use English to interact in the classroom	all
2.2—Students will use English to obtain, process, construct, and provide subject matter information in spoken and written form	all
2.3—Students will use appropriate learning strategies to construct and apply academic knowledge	all

Excerpt from

Robinson Crusoe

by Daniel Defoe

Nothing can describe the fear which I felt. I sank into the water. I swam very well. Yet I could not save myself from the waves long enough to draw a breath. First, the wave must carry me a long way towards the shore. Then it must spend itself and fall back. This happened over and over. It left me upon the land almost dry. But I was half dead with the water I had taken in.

I could think clearly enough that, seeing myself nearer the shore than I had hoped, I got to my feet. I tried to move towards the land as fast as I could. I did not want another wave to fall upon me. But I soon found it was impossible to avoid it. I saw the sea come after me. It was high as a hill and as angry as an enemy. I had no strength to fight it. My goal was to hold my breath and raise myself upon the water. I tried by swimming to keep breathing and to move myself towards the shore.

The next wave buried me twenty or thirty feet deep in its body. I could feel myself carried with great force and speed towards the shore. I held my breath and swam with all my might. I was ready to burst from holding my breath. Just then, I felt myself rising. Then my head and hands shot out above the surface of the water. It was less than two seconds of time that I could keep myself so. Still, it gave me relief. What is more, it gave me a breath and new courage.

Then I was covered again with water but not so long this time. When the water had spent itself and began to return, I moved forward. I felt ground under my feet! I stood still a few moments to catch my breath. The waters fell back from me. I ran with what strength I had towards the shore. But this did not save me from the sea. It came pouring in after me again. Twice more I was lifted up by the waves. I was carried forward again.

The last of these two waves had almost killed me. The sea smashed me against a rock. It hit with such force that I was left helpless. The blow had knocked the breath from me. If the wave had returned quickly, I would have drowned. But I recovered a little. Then the wave returned. Seeing that I would be covered again with the water, I held onto a piece of the rock. I held my breath, too.

These waves were nearer land. They were not as high as at first. I held on until the wave withdrew. Then I set out at run. The next wave went over me. But it did not carry me away. Nor was I pulled back. The next run I took, I got to the land. I climbed up onto the cliffs of the shore. I sat down. At last, I was out of the reach of the water.

Element Focus: Setting

Why do you think the author selected this setting?

Excerpt from

Robinson Crusoe

by Daniel Defoe

Nothing can describe the confusion which I felt as I sank into the water. I swam very well. Yet I could not save myself from the waves long enough to draw a breath. First, the wave, having carried me a long way towards the shore, must spend itself, then fall back. This left me upon the land almost dry, but half dead with the water I'd taken in.

I could think clearly enough that, seeing myself nearer the shore than I expected, I got to my feet. I tried to move towards the land as fast as I could before another wave should fall upon me. But I soon found it was impossible to avoid it. I saw the sea come after me as high as a hill and as furious as an enemy. I had no means or strength to fight it. My goal was to hold my breath and raise myself upon the water if I could. I tried by swimming to save my breathing and to move myself towards the shore.

The next wave that came upon me buried me twenty or thirty feet deep in its body. I could feel myself carried with a mighty force and speed towards the shore. I held my breath and swam forward with all my might. I was ready to burst from holding my breath. Just then, I felt myself rising. To my relief, I found my head and hands shoot out above the surface of the water. Even though it was not two seconds of time that I could keep myself so, it relieved me. It gave me a breath and new courage.

Then I was covered again with water but not so long this time. Finding the water had spent itself and began to return, I struck forward against the return of the waves. I felt ground under my feet! I stood still a few moments to catch my breath. The waters fell back from me. I then ran with what strength I had towards the shore. But this did not save me from the fury of the sea. It came pouring in after me again. Twice more I was lifted up by the waves and carried forward as before.

The last of these two waves had been nearly deadly to me. The sea smashed me against a rock. It hit with such force that I was left senseless and helpless. The blow had beaten the breath out of me. Had the wave returned again quickly, I would have drowned. But I recovered a little before the return of the wave. Seeing that I would be covered again with the water, I chose to grab onto a piece of the rock and hold my breath.

These waves were nearer land and thus not as high as at first. I held on until the wave withdrew. Then I set out at run. The next wave, though it went over me, did not carry me away. Nor was I pulled backwards. The next run I took, I reached the land. With great effort, I climbed up onto the cliffs of the shore. I sat down. At last, I was out of the reach of the water.

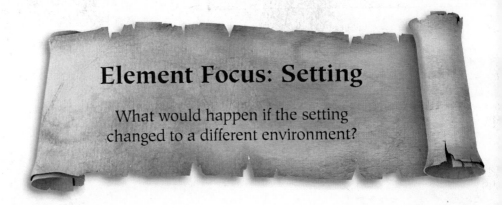

Element Focus: Setting

What would happen if the setting changed to a different environment?

#50983—*Leveled Texts for Classic Fiction: Adventure*

Excerpt from

Robinson Crusoe

by Daniel Defoe

||||||||||||||||||||||||||||||||||||||||||||||||||||||||||||||||||||||||||||||||||||||||||||||||||||||||||||||||||

Nothing can describe the confusion which I felt when I sank into the water. I swam very well, yet I could not deliver myself from the waves long enough to draw breath. First, the wave, having carried me a vast way towards the shore, must spend itself and then recede. This left me upon the land almost dry, but half dead with the water I'd taken in.

I had enough presence of mind that, seeing myself nearer the shore than I expected, I got upon my feet. I attempted to move towards the land as fast as I could before another wave should fall upon me again. But I soon found it was impossible to avoid it. I saw the sea come after me as high as a great hill and as furious as an enemy. I had no means or strength to contend with it. My objective was to hold my breath, and raise myself upon the water if I could. I attempted by swimming to preserve my breathing and move myself towards the shore.

The next wave that came upon me buried me twenty or thirty feet deep in its body. I could feel myself carried with a mighty force and swiftness towards the shore. I held my breath, and helped myself to swim forward with all my strength. Just when I was ready to burst with holding my breath, I felt myself rising. To my great relief, I found my head and hands shoot out above the surface of the water. Although it was not two seconds of time that I could keep myself so, it relieved me. It gave me a breath and new courage.

Then I was covered again with water but not so long. Finding the water had spent itself, and began to return, I struck forward against the return of the waves and felt ground under my feet! I stood still a few moments to recover my breath. The waters went from me. I then ran with what strength I had towards the shore. But this did not deliver me from the fury of the sea, which came pouring in after me again. Twice more I was lifted up by the waves and carried forward as before.

The last of these two waves had been nearly fatal to me, for the sea dashed me against a rock with such force that I was left senseless and helpless. The blow taken by my side had beaten the breath out of me. Had the wave returned again immediately, I would have drowned, but I recovered a little before the return of the wave. Seeing I should be covered again with the water, I decided to hold onto a piece of the rock, and hold my breath until the wave fell back.

Since these waves were nearer land and thus not as high as at first, I held on until the wave abated. Then I set out at run. The next wave, though it went over me, did not carry me away nor pull me backwards. The next run I took, I reached the land. With great effort, I climbed up the cliffs of the shore. I sat down, out of the reach of the water at last.

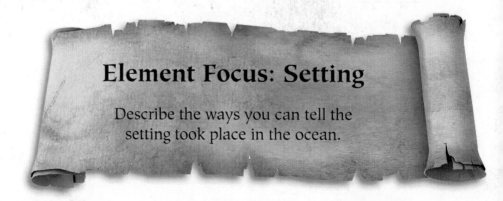

Element Focus: Setting

Describe the ways you can tell the setting took place in the ocean.

Excerpt from

Robinson Crusoe

by Daniel Defoe

||||||||||||||||||||||||||||||||||||||||||||||||||||||||||||||||||||||||||||||||||||||||||||||||||||||||||||||||||||||||||||||||||||||||||

Nothing can describe the confusion which I felt when I sank into the water. Although I swam very well, I could not deliver myself from the waves so as to draw breath, until that wave having carried me a vast way towards the shore, and having spent itself, receded. This left me upon the land almost dry, but half dead with the water I'd taken in.

I had enough presence of mind that seeing myself nearer the mainland than I expected, I got upon my feet, and endeavored to move towards the land as fast as I could before another wave should take me up again. But I soon found it was impossible to avoid it. I saw the sea come after me as high as a great hill, and as furious as an enemy. I had no means or strength to contend with it. My business was to hold my breath, and raise myself upon the water if I could; and so by swimming to preserve my breathing, and move myself towards the shore, if possible.

The next wave that came upon me buried me twenty or thirty feet deep in its body. I could feel myself carried with a mighty force and swiftness towards the shore. I held my breath, and assisted myself to swim forward with all my might. I was ready to burst with holding my breath, when, as I felt myself rising up. To my immediate relief, I found my head and hands shoot out above the surface of the water; and though it was not two seconds of time that I could keep myself so, it relieved me greatly, gave me breath and new courage.

Then I was covered again with water but not so long, and finding the water had spent itself, and began to return, I struck forward against the return of the waves, and felt ground with my feet! I stood still a few moments to recover my breath, and the waters went from me. I then ran with what strength I had further towards the shore. But this did not deliver me from the fury of the sea, which came pouring in after me again. Twice more I was lifted up by the waves and carried forward as before, the shore being flat.

The last of these two waves had been nearly fatal to me, for the sea dashed me against a piece of rock with such force that it left me senseless and helpless. The blow taken by my side beat the breath out of me. Had the wave returned again immediately, I would have drowned. But I recovered a little before the return of the wave, and seeing I should be covered again with the water, I resolved to hold fast onto a piece of the rock, and hold my breath, until the wave fell back.

Since these waves were nearer land and thus not as high as at first, I held on until the wave abated, and then set out at run. The next wave, though it went over me, did not carry me away nor pull me backwards. The next run I took, I got to the mainland. With great effort, I climbed up the cliffs of the shore and sat down, out of the reach of the water at last.

Element Focus: Setting

Why is the setting of the ocean important to the story?

Excerpt from

Hans Brinker

by Mary Mapes Dodge

It was a December morning long ago. Two children knelt upon the bank of a frozen canal in Holland. The sun had not yet risen. Near the horizon, the gray sky was split. Its edges shone red with the coming day. Most Hollanders were still asleep.

Now and then a woman, carrying a full basket upon her head, came skimming over the glassy surface of the canal. A boy, skating to his day's work in the town, looked toward the shivering pair as he flew past.

Meanwhile, with many a strong pull, the brother and sister were tying something to their feet. They were not skates, but clumsy pieces of wood. They were narrowed and smoothed at their lower edge, and pierced with holes. Strings of rawhide were threaded through the holes. The boy, Hans had made these odd-looking substitutes for skates. His mother was a poor woman. She was too poor to buy her children skates. Rough as these were, they had given the children many happy hours upon the ice. With cold, red fingers the children tugged at the strings. Their faces bent closely over their knees. They did not think about the iron blades they could not have.

In a moment, the boy arose. With a swing of his arms he said, "Come on, Gretel!" He skated across the canal.

"Wait, Hans," called his sister. "This foot is not well yet. The strings hurt me yesterday. Now I cannot bear having them tied in the same spot!"

 #50983—Leveled Texts for Classic Fiction: Adventure

"Tie them higher up," said Hans. He did not look at her as he did a wonderful twirl on the ice.

"How can I? The string is too short."

Hans mumbled under his breath that girls were troublesome. He skated back to Gretel.

"You are foolish to wear such shoes, Gretel. You have a leather pair. Even your wooden clogs would be better than these."

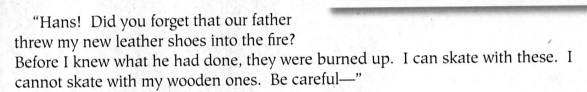

"Hans! Did you forget that our father threw my new leather shoes into the fire? Before I knew what he had done, they were burned up. I can skate with these. I cannot skate with my wooden ones. Be careful—"

Hans had taken a string from his pocket. He hummed as he knelt beside her. He fastened Gretel's skate with all the force of his strong young arm.

"Ow!" she cried in real pain.

Hans undid the string with an impatient jerk. He would have thrown it on the ground. But just then he saw a tear trickling down his sister's cheek.

"I'll fix it," he said, "but we must be quick. Mother will need us soon." Then he looked around him. He looked at the ground and at some bare tree branches above his head. Then he looked at the sky. It showed streaks of blue, red, and gold. He found nothing in any of these places to meet his need. But his face brightened. With the air of a fellow who knew just what to do, he took off his cap. He removed its torn lining. He folded it to form a smooth pad. He put it on top of Gretel's old shoe.

Element Focus: Setting

Why would the author select this setting?

#50983—*Leveled Texts for Classic Fiction: Adventure*

Excerpt from
Hans Brinker

by Mary Mapes Dodge

It was a bright December morning long ago. Two thinly clad children knelt upon the bank of a frozen canal in Holland. The sun had not yet risen. Yet the gray sky was parted near the horizon. Its edges shone red with the coming day. Most of the good Hollanders were still asleep.

Now and then a peasant woman, carrying a full basket upon her head, came skimming over the glassy surface of the canal, or a boy, skating to his day's work in the town, cast a glance toward the shivering pair as he flew past.

Meanwhile, with many a vigorous pull, the brother and sister seemed to be tying something to their feet—not skates, but clumsy pieces of wood. They were narrowed and smoothed at their lower edge, and pierced with holes. Strings of rawhide were threaded through the holes. The boy Hans had made these queer-looking substitutes for skates. His mother was a poor woman. She was too poor to buy her children skates. Rough as these were, they had given the children many happy hours upon the ice. With cold, red fingers our youngsters tugged at the strings. Their solemn faces bent closely over their knees. No thoughts of impossible iron blades came to dull their satisfaction.

In a moment, the boy arose. With a pompous swing of his arms and a careless, "Come on, Gretel," he glided easily across the canal.

"Wait, Hans," called his sister. "This foot is not well yet. The strings hurt me yesterday. Now I cannot bear having them tied in the same place!"

#50983—Leveled Texts for Classic Fiction: Adventure

"Tie them higher up, then," said Hans. Without looking at her, he did a wonderful twirl on the ice.

"How can I? The string is too short."

Mumbling under his breath that girls were troublesome, Hans steered toward Gretel.

"You are foolish to wear such shoes, Gretel. You have a stout leather pair. Even your wooden clogs would be better than these."

"Hans! Did you forget that our father threw my new leather shoes into the fire? Before I knew what he had done, they were all curled up in the midst of the burning peat. I can skate with these. I cannot skate with my wooden ones. Be careful now—"

Hans had taken a string from his pocket. He hummed a tune as he knelt beside her. He fastened Gretel's skate with all the force of his strong young arm.

"Ow!" she cried in real pain.

With an impatient jerk, Hans undid the string. He would have thrown it on the ground in true big-brother style. But just then he saw a tear trickling down his sister's cheek.

"I'll fix it," he said, "but we must be quick. Mother will need us soon." Then he glanced all about him, first at the ground, next at some bare willow branches above his head, and then at the sky, now showing streaks of blue, red, and gold. He found nothing in any of these places to meet his need. But his face suddenly brightened. With the air of a fellow who knew just what to do, he took off his cap. He removed its tattered lining. He adjusted it to form a smooth pad over the top of Gretel's worn-out shoe.

Element Focus: Setting

Explain why the characters fit well with this setting.

#50983—Leveled Texts for Classic Fiction: Adventure

Excerpt from

Hans Brinker

by Mary Mapes Dodge

On a bright December morning long ago, two thinly clad children knelt upon the bank of a frozen canal in Holland. The sun had not yet appeared. Yet the gray sky was parted near the horizon. Its edges shone crimson with the coming day. Most of the good Hollanders were still slumbering.

Now and then a peasant woman, poising a well-filled basket upon her head, came skimming over the glassy surface of the canal, or a boy, skating to his day's work in the town, cast a good-natured glance toward the shivering pair as he flew past.

Meanwhile, with many a vigorous pull, the brother and sister seemed to be fastening something to their feet—not skates, certainly, but clumsy pieces of wood. They were narrowed and smoothed at their lower edge, and pierced with holes, through which were threaded strings of rawhide. These queer-looking affairs had been made by the boy, Hans. His mother was a poor peasant woman. She was too poor to even think of buying her children skates. Rough as these were, they had given the children many happy hours upon the ice. Now, with cold, red fingers our youngsters tugged at the strings, their solemn faces bent closely over their knees. No vision of impossible iron blades came to dull the satisfaction glowing within.

In a moment, the boy arose and, with a pompous swing of his arms and a careless, "Come on, Gretel," he glided easily across the canal.

"Wait, Hans," called his sister plaintively. "This foot is not well yet. The strings hurt me yesterday. Now I cannot bear them having tied in the same place!"

     #50983—Leveled Texts for Classic Fiction: Adventure

"Tie them higher up, then," answered Hans. Without looking at her, he performed a wonderful twirl on the ice.

"How can I? The string is too short."

Mumbling under his breath that girls were troublesome, Hans steered toward Gretel.

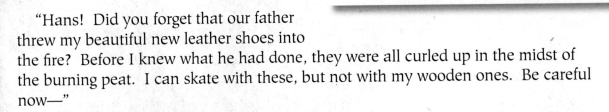

"You are foolish to wear such shoes, Gretel. You have a stout leather pair. Even your wooden clogs would be better than these."

"Hans! Did you forget that our father threw my beautiful new leather shoes into the fire? Before I knew what he had done, they were all curled up in the midst of the burning peat. I can skate with these, but not with my wooden ones. Be careful now—"

Hans had taken a string from his pocket. Humming a tune as he knelt beside her, he proceeded to fasten Gretel's skate with all the force of his strong young arm.

"Ow!" she cried in real pain.

With an impatient jerk, Hans unwound the string. He would have thrown it on the ground in true big-brother style, but just then he spied a tear trickling down his sister's cheek.

"I'll fix it—never fear," he said with sudden tenderness, "but we must be quick. Mother will need us soon." Then he glanced all about him, first at the ground, next at some bare willow branches above his head, and finally at the sky, now gorgeous with streaks of blue, crimson, and gold. He found nothing in any of these places to meet his need. But his face suddenly brightened as, with the air of a fellow who knew just what to do, he took off his cap. He removed its tattered lining and adjusted it to form a smooth pad over the top of Gretel's worn-out shoe.

Element Focus: Setting

What in the setting makes you feel cold?

Excerpt from

Hans Brinker

by Mary Mapes Dodge

On a bright December morning long ago, two thinly clad children knelt upon the bank of a frozen canal in Holland. The sun had not yet appeared, but the gray sky was parted near the horizon, and its edges shone crimson with the coming day. Most of the good Hollanders were still slumbering in beautiful repose.

Now and then some peasant woman, poising a well-filled basket upon her head, came skimming over the glassy surface of the canal, or a healthy boy, skating to his day's work in the town, cast a good-natured glance toward the shivering pair as he flew past.

Meanwhile, with many a vigorous pull, the brother and sister seemed to be fastening something to their feet—not skates, certainly, but clumsy pieces of wood narrowed and smoothed at their lower edge, and pierced with holes, through which were threaded strings of rawhide. These queer-looking affairs had been made by the boy Hans. His mother was a poor peasant woman, too poor to even think of buying skates for her children. Rough as these were, they had afforded the children many a happy hour upon the ice. Now, as with cold, red fingers our young Hollanders tugged at the strings—their solemn faces bent closely over their knees—no vision of impossible iron blades came to dull the satisfaction glowing within.

In a moment the boy arose and, with a pompous swing of his arms and a careless, "Come on, Gretel," glided easily across the canal.

"Wait, Hans," called his sister plaintively, "this foot is not well yet. The strings hurt me yesterday, and now I cannot bear them tied in the same place."

"Tie them higher up, then," answered Hans, as without looking at her, he performed a wonderful twirl on the ice.

"How can I? The string is too short."

Mumbling under his breath that girls were troublesome creatures, Hans steered toward Gretel.

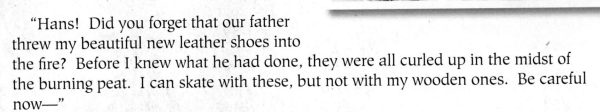

"You are foolish to wear such shoes, Gretel, when you have a stout leather pair. Your wooden clogs would be better than these."

"Hans! Did you forget that our father threw my beautiful new leather shoes into the fire? Before I knew what he had done, they were all curled up in the midst of the burning peat. I can skate with these, but not with my wooden ones. Be careful now—"

Hans had taken a string from his pocket. Humming a tune as he knelt beside her, he proceeded to fasten Gretel's skate with all the force of his strong young arm.

"Ow!" she cried in real pain.

With an impatient jerk, Hans unwound the string. He would have thrown it on the ground in true big-brother style, had he not just then spied a tear trickling down his sister's cheek.

"I'll fix it—never fear," he said with tenderness, "but we must be quick. Mother will need us soon." Then he glanced inquiringly about him, first at the ground, next at some bare willow branches above his head, and finally at the sky, now gorgeous with streaks of blue, crimson, and gold. Finding nothing in any of these places to meet his need, his face suddenly brightened as, with the air of a fellow who knew just what to do, he took off his cap and, removing its tattered lining, adjusted it to form a smooth pad over the top of Gretel's worn-out shoe.

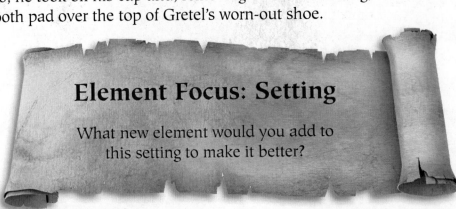

Element Focus: Setting

What new element would you add to this setting to make it better?

#50983—*Leveled Texts for Classic Fiction: Adventure*

The Adventures of Tom Sawyer

by Mark Twain

The minister spoke in a dull tone. The sermon was dull, too. Many heads began to nod. After a while, Tom thought of a treasure he had. He got out a box. In it was a large black beetle. Tom called it a "pinchbug." It had fierce jaws. The beetle grabbed his finger. Tom shook his hand. The beetle flew into the aisle. It landed on its back. The hurt finger went into the boy's mouth. The beetle lay there. It moved its legs. It could not turn over. Tom watched it. He longed for it. But it was out of his reach. Other people not interested in the sermon watched it, too.

Soon a poodle came along. He saw the beetle. His tail lifted and wagged. He studied the prize. He walked around it. He smelled it from a safe distance and walked around it again. He grew bolder and took a closer smell. Then he lifted his lip and made a snatch at it, just missing it. He made another and another. Then he laid down on his stomach with the beetle between his paws. He kept up

his experiments. He grew tired at last and then absent-minded. His head nodded. Little by little, his chin drooped lower. It touched the beetle, who grabbed it. There was a sharp yelp and a jerk of the poodle's head. The beetle fell a couple of yards away. It was on its back again. Nearby viewers shook with quiet joy. Some faces went behind fans and handkerchiefs. Tom was happy. The dog looked silly and probably felt so. There was anger in his heart, too. He wanted revenge. So he went to the beetle and began to attack it again. He jumped at it from every point. He landed with his forepaws within an inch of the bug. He made ever closer snatches at it with his teeth. He shook his head until his ears flapped.

But then the dog grew tired. He tried to amuse himself with a fly but lost interest. He followed an ant around, with his nose close to the floor. He quickly tired of that. Then he yawned and sighed. He forgot the beetle and sat down on it. There was a wild yelp of pain. The poodle went running up the aisle. The yelps continued, and so did the dog. He crossed the church in front of the altar. He flew down the other aisle. He crossed before the doors. At last the dog changed its course and sprang into its owner's lap. He flung it out an open window. The yelps of distress quickly thinned away. The yelps died in the distance.

By this time, the whole church was red-faced and suffocating with hidden laughter. The sermon came to a halt. The minister tried to restart. But his words were met with a smothered burst of giggles. It was a relief to all when he said the blessing.

Tom went home cheerful. He was thinking to himself that there was some satisfaction in a church service when there was a bit of variety to it. He had one negative thought. He was willing that the dog should play with his beetle. But he did not think it was right for him to run off with it.

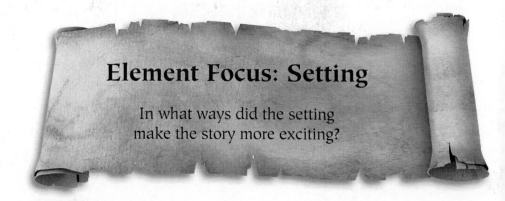

Element Focus: Setting

In what ways did the setting make the story more exciting?

Excerpt from

The Adventures of Tom Sawyer

by Mark Twain

The minister spoke in a dull tone. His sermon was so boring that many heads began to nod. After a while, Tom thought of a treasure he had. He got out a box. In it was a large black beetle. Tom called it a "pinchbug." It had fierce jaws. The beetle grabbed his finger. Tom shook his hand, and the beetle went flying into the aisle. It laid on its back. The hurt finger went into the boy's mouth. The beetle lay there working its helpless legs. It was unable to turn over. Tom eyed it and longed for it. But it was out of his reach. Other people not interested in the sermon eyed it, too.

Soon a poodle came idling along and spied the beetle. His drooping tail lifted and wagged. He studied the prize; walked around it; smelled at it from a safe distance; walked around it again; grew bolder, and took a closer smell. Then he lifted his lip and made a snatch at it, just missing it; made another, and another; laid down on his stomach with the beetle between his paws, and kept up his

experiments. He grew weary at last and then absent-minded. His head nodded. Little by little, his chin drooped lower. It touched the enemy, who seized it. There was a sharp yelp, a jerk of the poodle's head, and the beetle fell a couple of yards away. It lit on its back once more. Neighboring viewers shook with inward joy. Several faces went behind fans and handkerchiefs. Tom was happy. The dog looked foolish, and probably felt so. There was anger in his heart, too, and a desire for revenge. So he went to the beetle and began an attack on it again; jumping at it from every point. He landed with his forepaws within an inch of the creature, making ever closer snatches at it with his teeth, and shook his head until his ears flapped.

But the dog grew tired after a while. He tried to amuse himself with a fly but found no relief; followed an ant around, with his nose close to the floor, and quickly wearied of that. Then he yawned, sighed, forgot the beetle, and sat down on it. There was a wild yelp of pain, and the poodle went sailing up the aisle. The yelps continued, and so did the dog. He crossed the church in front of the altar and flew down the other aisle; he crossed before the doors. At last the sufferer changed its course and sprang into its master's lap. He flung it out an open window. The yelps of distress quickly thinned away and died in the distance.

By this time the whole church was red-faced and suffocating with hidden laughter. The sermon had come to a halt. The minister tried to restart, but his words were met with a smothered burst of unholy mirth. It was a genuine relief to everyone when he said the blessing.

Tom Sawyer went home quite cheerful. He was thinking to himself that there was some satisfaction about Sunday service when there was a bit of variety to it. He had one negative thought. He was willing that the dog should play with his pinchbug, but he did not think it was right for him to carry it off.

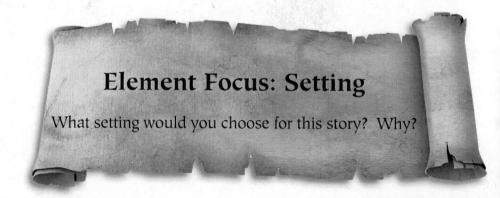

Element Focus: Setting

What setting would you choose for this story? Why?

The Adventures of Tom Sawyer

by Mark Twain

The minister droned monotonously through a sermon so dull that many a head began to nod. Presently Tom thought of a treasure he had and got out a box. In it was a large black beetle with formidable jaws—a "pinchbug." The beetle grabbed his finger. Tom shook his hand, and the beetle went floundering into the aisle and lit on its back, and the hurt finger went into the boy's mouth. The beetle lay there working its helpless legs, unable to turn over. Tom eyed it, and longed for it; but it was out of his reach. Other people uninterested in the sermon eyed it, too.

Presently a poodle came idling along. He spied the beetle; his drooping tail lifted and wagged. He surveyed the prize; walked around it; smelled at it from a safe distance; walked around it again; grew bolder, and took a closer smell; then lifted his lip and made a gingerly snatch at it, just missing it; made another, and another; laid down on his stomach with the beetle between his paws, and continued his experiments; grew weary at last, and then indifferent and absent-minded.

His head nodded, and little by little his chin descended. It touched the enemy, who seized it. There was a sharp yelp, a jerk of the poodle's head, and the beetle fell a couple of yards away and lit on its back once more. Neighboring spectators shook with a gentle inward joy, and several faces went behind fans and handkerchiefs. Tom was entirely happy. The dog looked foolish, and probably felt so; but there was resentment in his heart, too, and a craving for revenge. So he went to the beetle and began a wary attack on it again; jumping at it from every point, landing with his forepaws within an inch of the creature, making ever closer snatches at it with his teeth, and shaking his head until his ears flapped.

#50983—Leveled Texts for Classic Fiction: Adventure **51**

But he grew tired after a while; tried to amuse himself with a fly but found no relief; followed an ant around, with his nose close to the floor, and quickly wearied of that; yawned, sighed, forgot the beetle entirely, and sat down on it. Then there was a wild yelp of agony, and the poodle went sailing up the aisle. The yelps continued, and so did the dog; he crossed the church in front of the altar; he flew down the other aisle; he crossed before the doors. At last the frantic sufferer veered from its course and sprang into its master's lap. He flung it out an open window, and the yelps of distress quickly thinned away and died in the distance.

By this time the whole church was red-faced and suffocating with suppressed laughter, and the sermon had come to a dead standstill. The minister tried to restart but his words were met with a smothered burst of unholy mirth. It was a genuine relief to everyone when the blessing pronounced.

Tom Sawyer went home quite cheerful, thinking to himself that there was some satisfaction about Sunday service when there was a bit of variety in it. He had one negative thought: He was willing that the dog should play with his pinchbug, but he did not think it was right for him to carry it off.

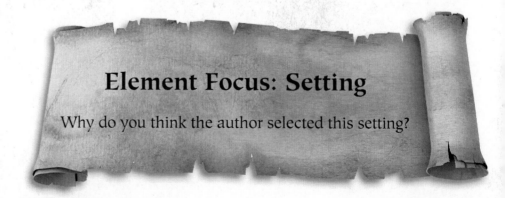

Element Focus: Setting

Why do you think the author selected this setting?

#50983—Leveled Texts for Classic Fiction: Adventure

Excerpt from

The Adventures of Tom Sawyer

by Mark Twain

The minister droned monotonously through a sermon so boring that many a head began to nod. Presently Tom remembered a treasure he had and got out a percussion-cap box. In it was an enormous black beetle with formidable jaws—a "pinchbug." The beetle seized his finger; Tom shook his hand, and the beetle went floundering into the aisle and lit on its back, and the injured finger went into the boy's mouth. The beetle lay there working its legs helplessly, unable to turn over. Tom eyed it, and longed for it; but it was out of his reach. Other people uninterested in the sermon also eyed the pinchbug.

Presently a poodle came idling along and spied the beetle; his drooping tail lifted and wagged. He surveyed the prize; walked around it; smelled it from a safe distance; walked around it again; grew bolder, and took a closer smell; then lifted his lip and made a gingerly snatch at it, just missing it; made another, and another; laid down on his stomach with the beetle between his paws, and continued his experiments; grew

weary at last, and then indifferent and absent-minded. His head nodded, and little by little his chin descended until it touched the enemy, who seized it. There was a sharp yelp, a jerk of the poodle's head, and the pinchbug fell a couple of yards away, on its back once more. Neighboring spectators shook with gentle inward laughter, several faces rapidly went behind fans and handkerchiefs, and Tom was entirely happy. The dog looked foolish, and probably felt so; but there was resentment in his heart, too, and a craving for revenge, so he went to the pinchbug and began a wary attack on it again; jumping at it from every angle, landing with his forepaws within an inch of the creature, making ever closer snatches at it with his teeth, and shaking his head until his ears flapped.

But the poodle grew tired after a while; tried to amuse himself with a fly but found no relief; followed an ant around with his nose close to the floor and quickly wearied of that; yawned, sighed, forgot the pinchbug entirely, and sat down on it. With wild yelps of agony, the poodle went sailing up the aisle; he crossed the church in front of the altar; he flew down the other aisle; he crossed before the doors. At last the frantic sufferer veered from its course and sprang into its master's lap. Embarrassed, he flung it out an open window, and its yelps of distress quickly thinned and died in the distance.

By this time the whole congregation was red-faced and suffocating with suppressed laughter, and the sermon had come to an absolute standstill. Although the minister valiantly tried to restart, his words were received with a smothered burst of unholy mirth. It was a genuine relief to everyone in the congregation when the final blessing was pronounced.

Tom Sawyer went home cheerful, thinking to himself that there was satisfaction about religious service when there was variety to it. He had but one negative thought: He was willing that the dog should play with his pinchbug, but he did not think it was fitting for him to carry it off.

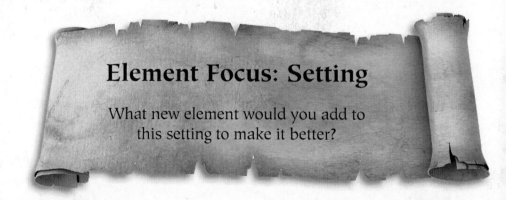

Element Focus: Setting

What new element would you add to this setting to make it better?

#50983—*Leveled Texts for Classic Fiction: Adventure*

Excerpt from

The Swiss Family Robinson

by Johann Wyss

I was eager to land the two barrels. They floated beside our boat. But I found that I could not get them up the bank on which we landed. I had to look for a better spot. As I did so, I was startled. I could hear Jack shouting for help. He sounded in great danger. He was at some distance. I hurried towards him with an axe in my hand.

The little fellow was in a deep pool. He stood screaming. As I drew closer, I saw that a huge lobster had his leg in its claw. Poor Jack was in a terrible fright. He kicked and kicked. Still his enemy hung on. I waded into the water. I grabbed the lobster firmly by the back and made it loosen its hold. We brought it to land.

Jack quickly recovered his good spirits. He was eager to take the prize to his mother. He caught the lobster in both hands. He instantly received such a nasty blow from its tail that he flung it down. He hit the animal with a large stone.

His display of temper upset me. "You are acting childish, my son," said I. "Do not strike an enemy for revenge, or when the enemy cannot defend itself. The lobster bit you. But you will eat the lobster! So the game is at least equal. Next time, be more kind."

Jack lifted the lobster again. He ran triumphantly towards the tent. "Mother! A lobster! A lobster, Ernest! Look here, Franz! Watch out! He will bite you! Where is Fritz?" All crowded around Jack and his prize. They remarked about its large size.

Ernest wanted his mother to make lobster soup by adding it to what she was boiling. She said she did not want to try such an experiment. She wanted to cook one dish at a time. I had noticed that the scene of Jack's adventure was a good place for getting the barrels on shore. I returned there. I succeeded in drawing them up on the beach. I set them on end and left them there.

On my return, I resumed the subject of Jack's lobster. I told him that he should have the claw all to himself to eat. I praised him, too, on being the first of us to discover something useful.

"As to that," said Ernest, "I found something good to eat, too. I just could not get at them without getting my feet wet."

"Pooh!" cried Jack, "I know what he saw. It was some nasty mussels! I saw them, too. Who wants to eat trash like that? Lobster for me!"

"I am sure they are oysters, not mussels," replied Ernest. "They were stuck to the rocks. They are oysters."

"Be good enough to fetch these oysters before our next meal," said I. "We must all push ourselves, Ernest. It is for the common good. Never let me hear you object to getting your feet wet. See how fast the sun has dried Jack and me."

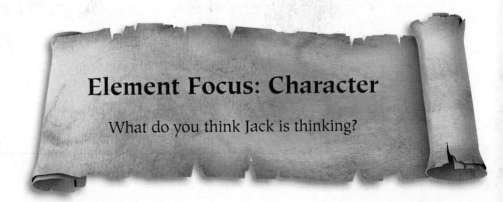

Element Focus: Character

What do you think Jack is thinking?

Excerpt from

The Swiss Family Robinson

by Johann Wyss

I was eager to land the two casks which floated beside our boat. In trying to do so, I found that I could not get them up the bank on which we landed. I had to look for a better spot. As I did, I was startled to hear Jack shouting for help. He sounded in great danger. He was at some distance, and I hurried towards him with an axe in my hand.

The little fellow stood screaming in a deep pool. As I drew closer, I saw that a huge lobster had caught his leg in its strong claw. Poor Jack was in a terrible fright. Kick as he would, his enemy hung on. I waded into the water, and seizing the lobster firmly by the back, managed to make it loosen its hold. We brought it to land.

Jack quickly recovered his spirits. He was anxious to take the prize to his mother and caught the lobster in both hands. He instantly received such a severe blow from its tail that he flung it down. He hit the creature with a large stone.

His display of temper upset me. "You are acting childish, my son," said I. "Never strike an enemy in a revengeful spirit, or when the enemy cannot defend itself. The lobster bit you. But you intend to eat the lobster! So the game is at least equal. Next time, be more prudent and more merciful."

Once more lifting the lobster, Jack ran triumphantly towards the tent. "Mother! A lobster! A lobster, Ernest! Look here, Franz! Watch out, he will bite you! Where is Fritz?" All came crowding around Jack and his prize. They remarked about its large size.

Ernest wanted his mother to make lobster soup by adding it to what she was boiling. She, however, declined any such experiment. She said she preferred cooking one dish at a time. Having noticed that the scene of Jack's adventure was a good place for getting my casks on shore, I returned there. I succeeded in drawing them up on the beach, where I set them on end and left them.

On my return, I resumed the subject of Jack's lobster. I told him that he should have the offending claw all to himself to eat. I congratulated him, too, on being the first of us to discover anything useful.

"As to that," said Ernest, "I found something very good to eat, too. I just could not get at them without wetting my feet."

"Pooh!" cried Jack, "I know what he saw—nothing but some nasty mussels! I saw them too. Who wants to eat trash like that? Lobster for me!"

"I am sure they are oysters, not mussels," replied Ernest. "They were stuck to the rocks. They are oysters."

"Be good enough, my young friend, to fetch a few specimens of these oysters before our next meal," said I. "We must all push ourselves, Ernest, for the common good. Never let me hear you object to getting your feet wet. See how fast the sun has dried Jack and me."

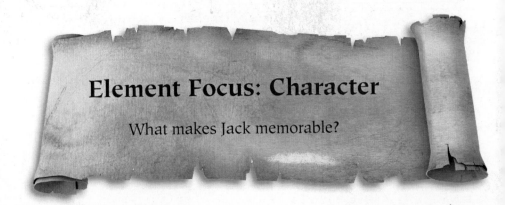

Element Focus: Character

What makes Jack memorable?

Excerpt from

The Swiss Family Robinson

by Johann Wyss

I was anxious to land the two casks which were floating alongside our boat, but on attempting to do so, I found that I could not get them up the bank on which we had landed, and was therefore obliged to look for a more convenient spot. As I did so, I was startled by hearing Jack shouting for help, as though in great danger. He was at some distance, and I hurried towards him with a hatchet in my hand.

The little fellow stood screaming in a deep pool. As I approached, I saw that a huge lobster had caught his leg in its powerful claw. Poor Jack was in a terrible fright; kick as he would, his enemy still clung on. I waded into the water, and seizing the lobster firmly by the back, managed to make it loosen its hold. We brought it safe to land.

Jack, having speedily recovered his spirits, and anxious to take such a prize to his mother, caught the lobster in both hands, but instantly received such a severe blow from its tail, that he flung it down, and passionately struck the creature with a large stone.

This display of temper upset me. "You are acting in a very childish way, my son," said I. "Never strike an enemy in a revengeful spirit, or when the enemy is unable to defend itself. The lobster, it is true, gave you a bite. But you intend to eat the lobster! So the game is at least equal. Next time, be more prudent and more merciful."

Once more lifting the lobster, Jack ran triumphantly towards the tent. "Mother, mother! A lobster! A lobster, Ernest! Look here, Franz! Mind, he'll bite you! Where's Fritz?" All came crowding around Jack and his prize, wondering at its unusual size.

#50983—Leveled Texts for Classic Fiction: Adventure

Ernest wanted his mother to make lobster soup by adding it to what she was now boiling. She, however, declined making any such experiment and said she preferred cooking one dish at a time. Having noticed that the scene of Jack's adventure was a convenient place for getting my casks on shore, I returned there and succeeded in drawing them up on the beach, where I set them on end and left them.

On my return, I resumed the subject of Jack's lobster. I told him that he should have the offending claw all to himself when it was ready to be eaten. I congratulated him, too, on being the first of us to discover anything useful.

"As to that," said Ernest, "I found something very good to eat, too, only I could not get at them without wetting my feet."

"Pooh!" cried Jack, "I know what he saw—nothing but some nasty mussels! I saw them too. Who wants to eat trash like that? Lobster for me!"

"I believe them to be oysters, not mussels," returned Ernest calmly. "They were stuck to the rocks, so I am sure they are oysters."

"Be good enough, my philosophical young friend, to fetch a few specimens of these oysters in time for our next meal," said I. "We must all exert ourselves, Ernest, for the common good. Never let me hear you object to wetting your feet. See how quickly the sun has dried Jack and me."

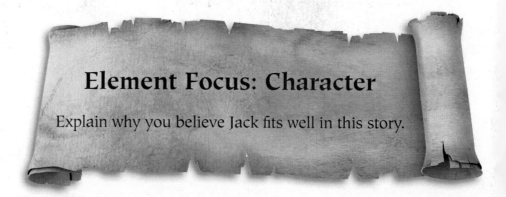

Element Focus: Character

Explain why you believe Jack fits well in this story.

Excerpt from

The Swiss Family Robinson

by Johann Wyss

I was anxious to land the two casks which were floating alongside our boat, but on attempting to do so, I found that I could not get them up the bank on which we had landed, and was therefore obliged to look for a more convenient spot. As I did so, I was startled by hearing Jack shouting for help, as though in great danger. He was at some distance, and I hurried towards him with a hatchet in my hand.

The little fellow stood screaming in a deep pool, and as I approached, I saw that a huge lobster had caught his leg in its powerful claw. Poor Jack was in a terrible fright; kick as he would, his enemy still clung on. I waded into the water, and seizing the lobster firmly by the back, managed to make it loosen its hold, and we brought it safe to land.

Jack, having speedily recovered his spirits, and anxious to take such a prize to his mother, caught the lobster in both hands, but instantly received such a severe blow from its tail, that he flung it down, and passionately struck the creature with a large stone.

This display of temper vexed me. "You are acting in a very childish way, my son," said I. "Never strike an enemy in a revengeful spirit, or when the enemy is unable to defend itself. The lobster, it is true, gave you a bite, but then you intend to eat the lobster. So the game is at least equal. Next time, be both more prudent and more merciful."

Once more lifting the lobster, Jack ran triumphantly towards the tent. "Mother, mother! A lobster! A lobster, Ernest! Look here, Franz! Mind, he'll bite you! Where's Fritz?"

All came crowding around Jack and his prize, wondering at its unusual size, and Ernest wanted his mother to make lobster soup by adding it to what she was now boiling. She, however, begged to decline making any such experiment and said she preferred cooking one dish at a time. Having remarked that the scene of Jack's adventure afforded a convenient place for getting my casks on shore, I returned there and succeeded in drawing them up on the beach, where I set them on end and left them.

On my return, I resumed the subject of Jack's lobster and told him he should have the offending claw all to himself when it was ready to be eaten, congratulating him on being the first of us to discover anything useful.

"As to that," said Ernest, "I found something very good to eat, too, only I could not get at them without wetting my feet."

"Pooh!" cried Jack, "I know what he saw—nothing but some nasty mussels—I saw them too. Who wants to eat trash like that? Lobster for me!"

"I believe them to be oysters, not mussels," returned Ernest calmly. "They were stuck to the rocks, so I am sure they are oysters."

"Be good enough, my philosophical young friend, to fetch a few specimens of these oysters in time for our next meal," said I. "We must all exert ourselves, Ernest, for the common good, and never let me hear you object to wetting your feet. See how quickly the sun has dried Jack and me."

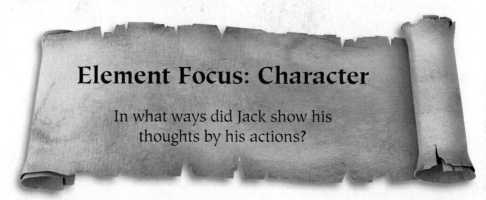

Element Focus: Character

In what ways did Jack show his thoughts by his actions?

Excerpt from

The Adventures of Huckleberry Finn

by Mark Twain

The Widow Douglas took me for her son. She said that she would civilize me. But it was rough for me living in the house all the time. The widow was an awful regular and decent in all her ways. When I couldn't stand it no longer, I ran off. I got into my old rags. I was free and satisfied. But Tom Sawyer hunted me up. He said he was going to start a band of robbers. I might join if I would go back to the widow and be respectable. And so I went back.

The widow, she cried over me. She called me a poor lost lamb. She called me a lot of other names, too, but she never meant no harm. She put me in them new clothes again. I couldn't do nothing but sweat and feel all cramped up. Well then, the old things started again. The widow rung a bell for supper. You had to come. When you got to the table, you couldn't get right to eating. You had to wait for the widow to grumble over the food, though there warn't anything the matter with it.

After supper she got out her book. She learned me about Moses and the Bulrushers. I was in a sweat to find out all about him. By and by she let slip that Moses had been dead a really long time. Then I didn't care no more about him. I don't take no stock in dead people.

Pretty soon I wanted to smoke. I asked the widow to let me, but she wouldn't. She said it was a mean practice. It wasn't clean. I must try to not do it any more. That is just the way with some people. They get down on a thing when they don't know nothing about it. Here she was bothering about Moses. He was no use to anybody, being dead. Yet she was finding fault with me for doing a thing that had some good in it.

Her sister was Miss Watson, a slim old maid with goggles. She had just come to live with her. She took a set at me now with a spelling book. She worked me middling hard for about an hour. Then the widow made her ease up. That was good because I couldn't have stood for it much longer. Then for an hour it was deadly dull. I was fidgety. Miss Watson would say, "Don't put your feet up there, Huckleberry"; and "Don't scrunch up like that, Huckleberry. Sit up straight!" Pretty soon she would say, "Don't yawn and stretch like that, Huckleberry! Why don't you try to behave?" Then she told me all about hell. I said I wished I was there. She got mad. But I didn't mean no harm. All I wanted was to go somewhere. All I wanted was a change. I warn't particular. She said it was wicked to say what I said. She wouldn't say it for the whole world. She was going to live so as to go to heaven. Well, I couldn't see no advantage in going where *she* was going. So I made up my mind I wouldn't try for it.

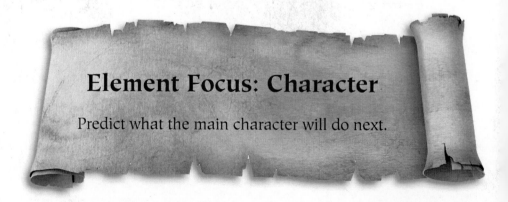

Element Focus: Character

Predict what the main character will do next.

#50983—*Leveled Texts for Classic Fiction: Adventure*

Excerpt from

The Adventures of Huckleberry Finn

by Mark Twain

The Widow Douglas took me for her son and said that she would civilize me. But it was rough living in the house all the time, considering how awful regular and decent the widow was in all her ways. So when I couldn't stand it no longer, I ran off. I got into my old rags and was free and satisfied. But Tom Sawyer hunted me up. He said he was going to start a band of robbers. I might join if I would go back to the widow and be respectable. And so I went back.

The widow, she cried over me and called me a poor lost lamb. She called me a lot of other names, too, but she never meant no harm. She put me in them new clothes again, and I couldn't do nothing but sweat and feel all cramped up. Well then, the old things commenced again. The widow rung a bell for supper, and you had to come. When you got to the table, you couldn't get right to eating. You had to wait for the widow to bow her head and grumble over the food, though there warn't anything the matter with it.

After supper she got out her book. She learned me about Moses and the Bulrushers. I was in a sweat to find out all about him. By and by she let slip that Moses had been dead a considerable long time, and then I didn't care no more about him because I don't take no stock in dead people.

Pretty soon I wanted to smoke and asked the widow to let me, but she wouldn't. She said it was a mean practice. It wasn't clean, and I must try to not do it any more. That is just the way with some people. They get down on a thing when they don't know nothing about it. Here she was bothering about Moses, who was no use to anybody, being dead, yet finding fault with me for doing a thing that had some good in it.

Her sister was Miss Watson, a slim old maid with goggles. She had just come to live with her. She took a set at me now with a spelling book. She worked me middling hard for about an hour. Then the widow made her ease up, which was good because I couldn't have stood for it much longer. Then for an hour it was deadly dull. I was fidgety. Miss Watson would say, "Don't put your feet up there, Huckleberry"; and "Don't scrunch up like that, Huckleberry—sit up straight!" Pretty soon she would say, "Don't yawn and stretch like that, Huckleberry! Why don't you try to behave?" Then she told me all about hell. I said I wished I was there. She got mad, but I didn't mean no harm. All I wanted was to go somewhere. All I wanted was a change; I warn't particular. She said it was wicked to say what I said. She wouldn't say it for the whole world; she was going to live so as to go to heaven. Well, I couldn't see no advantage in going where *she* was going. So I made up my mind I wouldn't try for it.

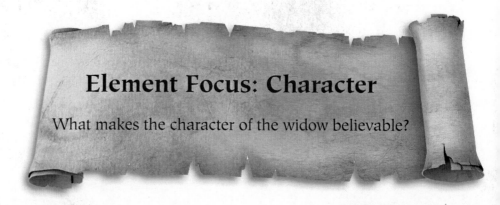

Element Focus: Character

What makes the character of the widow believable?

Excerpt from

The Adventures of Huckleberry Finn

by Mark Twain

The Widow Douglas she took me for her son and allowed as she would civilize me; but it was rough living in the house all the time, considering how dismal regular and decent the widow was in all her ways; and so when I couldn't stand it no longer, I ran off. I got into my old rags and was free and satisfied, but Tom Sawyer hunted me up and said he was going to start a band of robbers, and I might join if I would go back to the widow and be respectable. And so I went back.

The widow, she cried over me, and called me a poor lost lamb, and she called me a lot of other names, too, but she never meant no harm. She put me in them

new clothes again, and I couldn't do nothing but sweat and feel all cramped up. Well then, the old things commenced again. The widow rung a bell for supper, and you had to come. When you got to the table you couldn't get right to eating, but you had to wait for the widow to tuck down her head and grumble over the vittles, though there warn't anything the matter with them.

After supper she got out her book and learned me about Moses and the Bulrushers, and I was in a sweat to find out all about him. By and by she let out that Moses had been dead a considerable long time, so then I didn't care no more about him because I don't take no stock in dead people.

Pretty soon I wanted to smoke, and asked the widow to let me, but she wouldn't. She said it was a mean practice and wasn't clean, and I must try to not do it any more. That is just the way with some people; they get down on a thing when they don't know nothing about it. Here she was bothering about Moses, who was no use to anybody, being dead, yet finding fault with me for doing a thing that had some good in it.

Her sister, Miss Watson, a slim old maid with goggles, had just come to live with her, and took a set at me now with a spelling book. She worked me middling hard for about an hour, and then the widow made her ease up, which was good because I couldn't have stood for it much longer. Then for an hour it was deadly dull, and I was fidgety. Miss Watson would say, "Don't put your feet up there, Huckleberry"; and "Don't scrunch up like that, Huckleberry—sit up straight"; and pretty soon she would say, "Don't yawn and stretch like that, Huckleberry! Why don't you try to behave?" Then she told me all about hell, and I said I wished I was there. She got mad, but I didn't mean no harm. All I wanted was to go somewhere—all I wanted was a change; I warn't particular. She said it was wicked to say what I said; said she wouldn't say it for the whole world; she was going to live so as to go to heaven. Well, I couldn't see no advantage in going where *she* was going, so I made up my mind I wouldn't try for it.

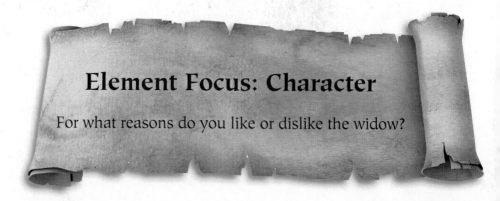

Element Focus: Character

For what reasons do you like or dislike the widow?

Excerpt from

The Adventures of Huckleberry Finn

by Mark Twain

||||||||||||||||||||||||||||||||||||||||||||||||||||||||||||||||||||||||||||||||||||||||||||||||||||||||||||||||||||||||||||||||||||

The Widow Douglas she took me for her son and allowed as she would civilize me; but it was rough living in the house all the time, considering how dismal regular and decent the widow was in all her ways; and so when I couldn't stand it no longer, I ran away. I put on my old rags and laid behind the hogshead and was free and satisfied until Tom Sawyer hunted me up and said he was going to start a band of robbers, and I might join if I would go back to the widow and be respectable, and so I returned.

Then the widow, she cried over me, and called me her poor lost lamb, and she called me a lot of other names, too, but she never meant no harm. She put me in them new clothes again, and I couldn't do nothing but sweat and feel all cramped up. Well then, all the old agonies commenced again. The widow rung a bell for supper, and you had to come. When you got to the table you couldn't get right to eating, but you had to wait for the widow to tuck down her head and grumble over the vittles, though there warn't anything the matter with them.

After supper the widow got out her book and learned me about Moses and the Bulrushers, and I was in a sweat to find out all about him. By and by she let loose that Moses had been dead a considerable long time, so then I didn't care no more about him because I don't take no stock in dead people.

Pretty soon I wanted to smoke, and asked the widow to let me, but she wouldn't. She said it was a mean practice and wasn't clean, and I must try to not do it any more. That is just the way with some people; they get down on a thing when they don't know nothing about it. Here she was bothering about Moses, who was no use to anybody, being dead, yet finding fault with me for doing a thing that had some good in it.

Her sister, Miss Watson, a slender old maid with goggles, had just come to live with her, and took a set at me now with a spelling book. She worked me middling hard for about an hour, and then the widow made her ease up, which was good because I couldn't have stood for it much longer. Then for an hour it was so deadly dull I was fidgety, and Miss Watson would say, "Don't put your feet up there, Huckleberry"; and "Don't scrunch up like that, Huckleberry—sit up straight"; and pretty soon she would say, "Don't yawn and stretch like that, Huckleberry—why don't you try to behave?" Then she told me all about hell, and I said I wished I was there. She got mad, but I didn't mean no harm: All I wanted was to go somewhere—I wanted a change; I warn't particular. She said it was wicked to say what I said; said she wouldn't say it for the whole world; she was going to live so as to go to heaven. Well, I couldn't see no advantage in going where *she* was going, so I made up my mind I wouldn't try for it.

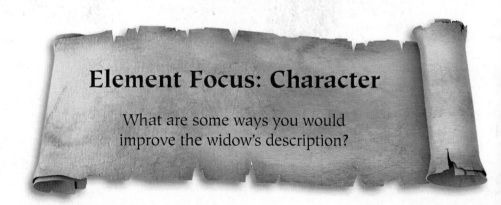

Element Focus: Character

What are some ways you would improve the widow's description?

#50983—*Leveled Texts for Classic Fiction: Adventure*

Excerpt from

The Railway Children

by E. Nesbit

Peter had a birthday. It was his tenth. One of his gifts was a model engine. The other gifts had charm. But the engine had more charm than all of them. Its charm lasted for three days. Then, the engine broke with a bang. James, the family's dog, was afraid. He ran off. He did not come back for days. All the Noah's Ark people were in the engine's tender. They were broken to bits. Nothing else was hurt except the little engine and Peter's feelings.

His sisters said he cried. But boys of ten do not cry. Peter said that his eyes were red because he had a cold. This turned out to be true. The next day he had to go to bed and stay there. Mother began to fear that he had the measles. Then, he sat up in bed. He said, "I hate gruel, barley, bread, and milk! I want to get up. I want to have something REAL to eat."

"What would you like?" Mother asked.

"A pigeon-pie," said Peter. "A big pigeon-pie."

So Mother asked the cook to make a big pigeon-pie. Peter ate it. Then, his cold was better.

Father had been away. He was gone for three or four days. Peter's hopes for mending his ruined engine were set on his Father. Father was clever. He could fix all sorts of things. He had often been a doctor for the wooden rocking-horse. Once he had saved its life when no one else could. The poor animal was given up for lost. Even the carpenter said he did not see what he could do to fix it. Father had fixed the doll's cradle when no one else could. And with a little glue and some bits of wood, he made all the Noah's Ark beasts as strong as ever.

Peter showed uncommon and heroic unselfishness. He did not say anything about his engine. He waited until after Father had his dinner and smoked his cigar. The unselfishness was Mother's idea. But it was Peter who did it. It took a lot of patience, too. At last Mother said to Father, "Now, if you're quite rested and comfortable, we want to tell you about the great railway accident. We need your advice."

"All right," said Father, "fire away!"

So then Peter fetched what was left of his engine. He told the sad tale.

"Hmmm," said Father. He had looked the engine over carefully.

The three children held their breaths. "Is there NO hope?" said Peter, in a low, unsteady voice.

"Hope? Tons of it," said Father. "But it will need more than hope. It needs a bit of solder and a new valve. I think we will keep it for a rainy day. I will do it on Saturday afternoon. You shall all help me."

"CAN girls fix engines?" Peter asked.

"Of course they can. Girls are just as clever as boys. Don't you forget it! Would you like to drive a train, Phyllis?"

"Drive a train? My face would always be dirty, wouldn't it?" said Phyllis, with no joy. "And I bet I would break something."

"I would love it," said Roberta with delight. "Do you think I could when I'm grown up, Daddy? Maybe even be a stoker?"

"You mean a fireman," said Daddy. He looked at the bottom of the Engine. "Well, if you still want to, when you are grown up, we will see about making you a fire-woman!"

Element Focus: Character

How might you have done things differently from how Peter did?

Excerpt from

The Railway Children

by E. Nesbit

Peter had a birthday. It was his tenth. Among his presents was a perfect model engine. The other presents had charm. But the engine had more charm than all of the others. Its charm lasted in its full perfection for three days. Then, the engine suddenly went off with a bang. James, the family's hound, was so afraid that he ran away. He did not come back for days. All the Noah's Ark people were sitting in the engine's tender. They were broken to bits. Nothing else was hurt except the poor little engine and Peter's feelings.

His sisters said he cried. Of course boys of ten do not cry, however awful the tragedies they must face. He said that his eyes were red because he had a cold. This turned out to be true. The next day he had to go to bed and stay there. Mother began to fear that he might be sick with the measles. Suddenly he sat up in bed and said, "I hate gruel, barley, bread, and milk! I want to get up and have something REAL to eat."

"What would you like?" Mother asked.

"A pigeon-pie," said Peter eagerly. "A very large pigeon-pie."

So Mother asked the cook to make a large pigeon-pie. After Peter ate it, his cold was better.

Father had been away in the country. He was gone for three or four days. All Peter's hopes for mending his ruined engine were fixed on his Father. Father was very clever. He could mend all sorts of things. He had often been a veterinarian to the wooden rocking-horse. Once he had saved its life when all human help was despaired of. The poor creature was given up for lost. Even the carpenter said he didn't see what he could do to fix it. Father had mended the doll's cradle when no one else could. And with a little glue and some bits of wood and a pen-knife he made all the Noah's Ark beasts as strong as ever they were.

Peter, with uncommon and heroic unselfishness, did not say anything about his engine. He waited until after Father had eaten his dinner and smoked his cigar. The unselfishness was Mother's idea. But it was Peter who carried it out. It took a lot of patience, too. At last Mother said to Father, "Now, dear, if you're quite rested and comfortable, we want to tell you about the great railway accident. We need to ask your advice."

"All right," said Father, "fire away!"

So then Peter fetched what was left of his engine. He told the sad tale.

"Hmmm," said Father, when he had looked the engine over carefully.

The three children held their breaths. "Is there NO hope?" said Peter, in a low, unsteady voice.

"Hope? Tons of it," said Father cheerfully. "But it'll want something besides hope—a bit of solder and a new valve. I think we'd better keep it for a rainy day. I'll give up Saturday afternoon to it. You shall all help me."

"CAN girls mend engines?" Peter asked doubtfully.

"Of course they can. Girls are just as clever as boys, and don't you forget it! How would you like to be an engineer, Phyllis?"

"Drive the engine? My face would always be dirty, wouldn't it?" said Phyllis, without enthusiasm. "And I think I would break something."

"I would just love it," said Roberta with delight. "Do you think I could when I'm grown up, Daddy? Maybe even be a stoker?"

"You mean a fireman," said Daddy. He looked at the underside of the Engine. "Well, if you still want to, when you're grown up, we'll see about making you a fire-woman!"

Element Focus: Character

What makes Peter believable?

#50983—*Leveled Texts for Classic Fiction: Adventure*

Excerpt from

The Railway Children

by E. Nesbit

Peter had a birthday—his tenth—and among his presents was a perfect model engine. The other presents were full of charm, but the engine had more charm than all of the others. Its charm lasted in its full perfection for three days. Then, the engine suddenly went off with a bang. James, the family's hound, was so terrified that he ran away and did not come back for days. All the Noah's Ark people who were sitting in the engine's tender were broken to bits. Nothing else was damaged except the poor little engine and Peter's feelings.

His sisters said he cried over it, but of course boys of ten do not cry, however awful the tragedies which darken their lives. He said that his eyes were red because he had a cold. This turned out to be true as the next day he had to go to bed and stay there. Mother began to fear that he might be sick with the measles when suddenly he sat up in bed and said, "I hate gruel, barley, bread, and milk! I want to get up and have something REAL to eat."

"What would you like?" Mother asked.

"A pigeon-pie," said Peter eagerly. "A very large pigeon-pie."

So Mother asked the cook to make a large pigeon-pie, and after Peter ate some of it, his cold was better.

Father had been away in the country for three or four days. All Peter's hopes for the curing of his ruined engine were fixed on his Father. Father was most wonderfully clever. He could mend all sorts of things. He had often acted as veterinary surgeon to the wooden rocking-horse. Once he had saved its life when all human aid was despaired of, and the poor creature was given up for lost. Even the carpenter said he didn't see how he could do anything to fix it. It was Father who mended the doll's cradle when no one else could. With a little glue and some bits of wood and a pen-knife, he made all the Noah's Ark beasts as strong as ever, if not stronger.

Peter, with uncharacteristic and heroic unselfishness, did not say anything about his engine. He waited until after Father had eaten his dinner and smoked his after-dinner cigar. The unselfishness was Mother's idea. But it was Peter who carried it out, and he needed a good deal of patience, too. At last Mother said to Father, "Now, dear, if you're quite rested and comfortable, we want to tell you about the great railway accident, and ask your advice."

"All right," said Father, "fire away!"

So then Peter told the sad tale, and fetched what was left of his engine.

"Hmmm," said Father, when he had looked the engine over very carefully.

The three children held their breaths. "Is there NO hope?" said Peter, in a low, unsteady voice.

"Hope? Tons of it," said Father cheerfully; "but it'll want something besides hope—a bit of solder and a new valve. I think we'd better keep it for a rainy day. I'll give up Saturday afternoon to it. You shall all help me."

"CAN girls actually mend engines?" Peter asked doubtfully.

"Of course they can. Girls are just as clever as boys, and don't you forget it! How would you like to be an engineer, Phyllis?"

"Drive the engine? My face would always be dirty, wouldn't it?" said Phyllis, very unenthusiastically. "And I imagine I would break something."

"I would just love it," said Roberta with delight. "Do you think I could when I'm grown up, Daddy? Maybe even be a stoker?"

"You mean a fireman," said Daddy, looking at the underside of the Engine. "Well, if you still want to, when you're grown up, we'll see about making you a fire-woman!"

Element Focus: Character

What are some possible explanations for how Peter resolved the situation?

Excerpt from
The Railway Children

by E. Nesbit

Peter had a birthday—his tenth—and among his presents was an impeccable model engine. The other presents were full of appeal, but the engine had more charisma than all of the others. Its charm lasted in its full perfection for precisely three days. Then, the engine suddenly went off with a bang. James, the family's hound, was so frightened that he ran away and did not come back for days. All the Noah's Ark people who were sitting in the engine's tender were broken to bits, but nothing else was damaged except the poor little engine and Peter's feelings.

His sisters said he bawled over it, but of course boys of ten do not cry, however terrible the tragedies which darken their lives. He said that his eyes were red because he had a cold, and this turned out to be accurate, as the next day he had to go to bed and remain there. Mother began to fear that he might be sick with the measles, when suddenly he sat up in bed and said, "I hate gruel, barley, bread, and milk! I want to get up and have something REAL to eat."

"What would you like?" Mother questioned.

"A pigeon-pie," said Peter enthusiastically, "a very large pigeon-pie."

So Mother asked the cook to make a large pigeon-pie, and after Peter consumed some of it, his cold improved.

Father had been away in the country for three or four days. All Peter's expectations for the curing of his afflicted engine were fixed on his Father, for Father was most wonderfully astute. He could mend all sorts of things. He had often acted as veterinary surgeon to the wooden rocking-horse; once he had saved its life when all human aid was despaired of, and the poor creature was given up for lost, and even the carpenter said he didn't see how he could do anything. It was Father who mended the doll's cradle when no one else could; and with a little glue and some bits of wood and a pen-knife, he made all the Noah's Ark beasts as strong as ever they were, if not stronger.

Peter, with uncharacteristic and heroic unselfishness, did not say anything about his engine until after Father had eaten his dinner and smoked his after-dinner cigar. The unselfishness was Mother's idea—but it was Peter who carried it out, and he needed a decent deal of patience, too. At last Mother said to Father, "Now, dear, if you're quite rested and comfortable, we want to tell you about the great railway accident, and ask your advice."

"All right," said Father, "fire away!"

So then Peter told the despondent tale, and fetched what was left of his engine.

"Hmmm," said Father, when he had observed the engine over very cautiously.

The three children held their breaths. "Is there NO hope?" said Peter, in a low, unsteady voice.

"Hope? Tons of it," said Father optimistically; "but it'll want something besides hope—a bit of solder and a new valve. I think we'd better keep it for a rainy day. I'll give up Saturday afternoon to it, and you shall all help me."

"CAN girls actually mend engines?" Peter asked doubtfully.

"Of course they can. Girls are just as ingenious as boys, and don't you forget it! How would you like to be an engineer, Phyllis?"

"Drive the engine? My face would always be filthy, wouldn't it?" said Phyllis, very unenthusiastically, and I imagine I would break something."

"I would just love it," said Roberta delightedly. "Do you think I could when I'm grown up, Daddy? Maybe even be a stoker?"

"You mean a fireman," said Daddy, examining the underside of the Engine. "Well, if you still desire it, when you're grown up, we'll see about making you a fire-woman!"

Element Focus: Character

For what reasons do you like or dislike Peter?

Rebecca of Sunnybrook Farm

by Kate Douglas Wiggin

Rebecca would ask the teacher for a drink. Then, she would walk to the water pail. It was in the corner. She would drink from the dipper. Samuel often went to drink after her. Drinking next made him feel close to her. And there was the joy of seeing her in passing. He would see the cold look in her lovely eyes.

The day was warm. Rebecca was thirsty. She asked for a third time to drink at the common pail. Miss Dearborn nodded "yes." Yet she lifted her eyebrows as Rebecca came near her desk. The girl set down the dipper. Samuel raised his hand. Miss Dearborn nodded again.

"What is wrong, Rebecca?" she asked.

"I had salted fish for breakfast," said Rebecca.

There was nothing funny about her reply. It was a fact. But a giggle ran through the school. Miss Dearborn's face turned red.

"Stand by the pail, Rebecca. It may end your thirst."

Rebecca's heart fluttered. She was to stand in the corner by the water pail! All the students stared at her! She moved a step closer to her seat. Miss Dearborn spoke again. Her voice was more firm.

"Stand by the pail, Rebecca! Samuel, how many times have you asked for water today?"

"This is the f-f-fourth."

"Do not touch the dipper, please. The whole school has done nothing but drink this afternoon. It has had no time to study. Did you have something salty for breakfast, Samuel?" Miss Dearborn asked the question with sarcasm.

#50983—Leveled Texts for Classic Fiction: Adventure

"I had salted fish, like Reb-b-becca." (Quiet giggles by the students.)

"I judged so. Stand by the other side of the pail, Samuel."

Rebecca's head was bowed. She felt shame. Life looked too black to be endured. To be punished was bad enough. To be corrected with Samuel Simpson was just awful.

Each day school ended with singing. Minnie chose the song "Shall We Gather at the River?" The song seemed to be a secret message about the situation. For each chorus, the students sang loudly:

"Shall we gather at the river, the beautiful, the beautiful river?"

Miss Dearborn looked at Rebecca. The child's head was bent. Her face was pale. Two red spots glowed on her cheeks. Tears hung on her lashes. Her breath came and went quickly.

The first song ended. "Go to your seat, Rebecca," said Miss Dearborn. "Samuel, stay there. Students, I made Rebecca stand by the pail to stop this habit of constant drinking. It is no more than a silly desire to walk to and fro. Each time Rebecca has asked for a drink today, the whole school has gone to the pail. She is really thirsty. I should have punished *you* for following her example, not her for setting it. What shall we sing now, Alice?"

"The 'Old Oaken Pail,' please."

"Choose something dry, Alice. Change the subject. The 'Star-Spangled Banner' if you like or anything else."

Rebecca sank into her seat. She took the singing book from her desk. Miss Dearborn's speech had made her feel a little better.

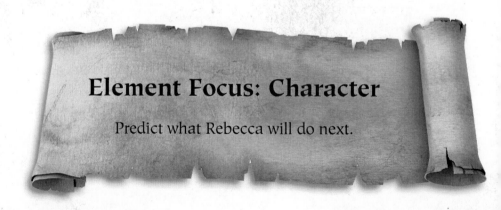

Element Focus: Character

Predict what Rebecca will do next.

Excerpt from

Rebecca of Sunnybrook Farm

by Kate Douglas Wiggin

After getting permission, Rebecca would walk to the water pail in the corner. She would drink from the dipper. Samuel often left his seat to go and drink after her. There was something intimate about drinking next. Also, there was the joy of meeting her in passing and receiving a cold look from her lovely eyes.

One warm day Rebecca was very thirsty. When she asked a third time to drink at the common pail, Miss Dearborn nodded "yes." Yet she lifted her eyebrows as Rebecca neared her desk. As the girl replaced the dipper, Samuel promptly raised his hand. Miss Dearborn nodded wearily.

"What is wrong with you, Rebecca?" she asked.

"I had salted fish for breakfast," answered Rebecca.

There was nothing funny about this reply. It was a statement of a fact. But an irrepressible giggle ran through the school. Miss Dearborn's face turned red.

"I think you had better stand by the pail, Rebecca. It may help to end your thirst."

Rebecca's heart fluttered. She was to stand in the corner by the water pail! All the students stared at her! She moved a step closer to her seat. She was stopped by Miss Dearborn's command in a still firmer voice.

"Stand by the pail, Rebecca! Samuel, how many times have you asked for water today?"

"This is the f-f-fourth."

"Don't touch the dipper, please. The whole school has done nothing but drink this afternoon. It has had no time to study. I suppose you had something salty for breakfast, Samuel?" asked Miss Dearborn with sarcasm.

"I had salted fish, like Reb-b-becca." (Quiet giggles by the students.)

"I judged so. Stand by the other side of the pail, Samuel."

Rebecca's head was bowed in shame. Life looked too black a thing to be endured. The punishment was bad enough. To be corrected with Samuel Simpson was beyond endurance.

Singing was how school ended each day. Minnie chose "Shall We Gather at the River?" The song seemed to be a secret message about the situation. The students shouted the chorus with great energy:

"Shall we gather at the river, the beautiful, the beautiful river?"

Miss Dearborn looked at Rebecca's bent head. The child's face was pale. Two red spots glowed on her cheeks. Tears hung on her lashes. Her breath came and went quickly.

"You may go to your seat, Rebecca," said Miss Dearborn at the end of the first song. "Samuel, stay where you are. Students, I asked Rebecca to stand by the pail to break this habit of constant drinking. It is no more than a silly desire to walk to and fro. Each time Rebecca has asked for a drink today, the whole school has gone to the pail one after another. She is really thirsty. I dare say I ought to have punished *you* for following her example, not her for setting it. What shall we sing now, Alice?"

"The 'Old Oaken Pail,' please."

"Think of something dry, Alice. Change the subject. The 'Star-Spangled Banner' if you like or anything else."

Rebecca sank into her seat. She pulled the singing book from her desk. Miss Dearborn's speech had lifted some of the weight from her heart.

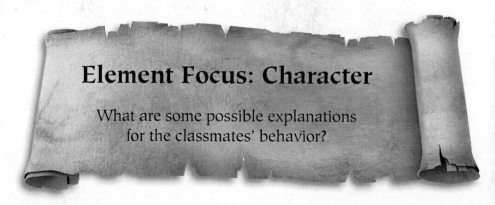

Element Focus: Character

What are some possible explanations
for the classmates' behavior?

Excerpt from

Rebecca of Sunnybrook Farm

by Kate Douglas Wiggin

When, having obtained permission, Rebecca walked to the water bucket in the corner and drank from the dipper, Samuel often left his seat to go and drink after her. It was not only that there was something intimate about drinking next, but there was the joy of meeting her in passing and receiving a cold look from her wonderful eyes.

One warm summer day Rebecca was very thirsty. When she asked a third time for permission to drink at the common bucket, Miss Dearborn nodded "yes," yet lifted her eyebrows unpleasantly as Rebecca neared her desk. As she replaced the dipper, Samuel promptly raised his hand. Miss Dearborn nodded her head wearily.

"What is the matter with you, Rebecca?" she asked.

"I had salted fish for breakfast," answered Rebecca.

There was nothing humorous about this reply; it was a statement of a fact, but an irrepressible titter ran through the school. Miss Dearborn's face flushed.

"I think you had better stand by the bucket, Rebecca. It may help you to control your thirst."

Rebecca's heart fluttered. She was to stand in the corner by the water bucket and be stared at by all the students! She moved a step nearer her seat, but was stopped by Miss Dearborn's command in a still firmer voice.

"Stand by the pail, Rebecca! Samuel, how many times have you asked for water today?"

"This is the f-f-fourth."

"Don't touch the dipper, please. The school has done nothing but drink this afternoon. It has had no time to study. I suppose you had something salty for breakfast, Samuel?" asked Miss Dearborn with sarcasm.

"I had salted fish, j-just like Reb-b-becca." (Quiet giggles by the students.)

"I judged so. Stand by the other side of the bucket, Samuel."

Rebecca's head was bowed with shame, and life looked too black a thing to be endured. The punishment was bad enough, but to be corrected with Samuel Simpson was beyond human endurance.

Singing was the last activity of the day, and Minnie chose "Shall We Gather at the River?" The song seemed to hold some secret, subtle association with the situation. The students shouted the choral invitation again and again with great energy:

"Shall we gather at the river, the beautiful, the beautiful river?"

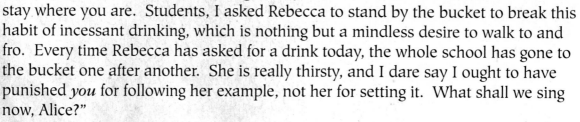

Miss Dearborn looked at Rebecca's bent head. The child's face was pale save for two red spots glowing on her cheeks. Tears hung on her lashes, and her breath came and went quickly.

"You may go to your seat, Rebecca," said Miss Dearborn at the end of the first song. "Samuel, stay where you are. Students, I asked Rebecca to stand by the bucket to break this habit of incessant drinking, which is nothing but a mindless desire to walk to and fro. Every time Rebecca has asked for a drink today, the whole school has gone to the bucket one after another. She is really thirsty, and I dare say I ought to have punished *you* for following her example, not her for setting it. What shall we sing now, Alice?"

"The 'Old Oaken Bucket,' please."

"Think of something dry, Alice, and change the subject. The 'Star-Spangled Banner' if you like or anything else."

Rebecca sank into her seat and pulled the singing book from her desk. Miss Dearborn's public explanation had lifted some of the weight from her heart.

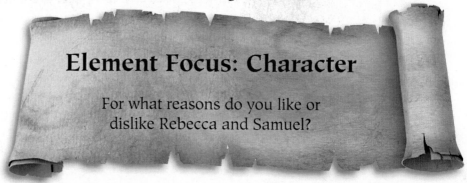

Element Focus: Character

For what reasons do you like or dislike Rebecca and Samuel?

Excerpt from

Rebecca of Sunnybrook Farm

by Kate Douglas Wiggin

||||||||||||||||||||||||||||||||||||||||||||||||||||||||||||||||||||||||||||||||||||||||||||||||||||||||||||

When, after obtaining permission, Rebecca walked to the water bucket in the corner and drank from the dipper, Samuel frequently left his seat to go and drink after her. It was not only that there was something intimate about drinking next, but there was the delight of meeting her in passing and receiving a cold look from her wonderful eyes.

One humid summer day Rebecca was very thirsty, so when she asked a third time for permission to drink at the common bucket, Miss Dearborn nodded "yes," yet lifted her eyebrows unpleasantly as Rebecca approached her desk. As Rebecca replaced the dipper, Samuel promptly raised his hand, and Miss Dearborn nodded her assent wearily.

"What is the matter with you, Rebecca?" she asked.

"I had salted fish for breakfast," answered Rebecca.

There was nothing humorous about this reply; it was merely a statement of a fact, but an irrepressible titter ran through the school. Miss Dearborn's face flushed scarlet.

"I think you had better stand by the bucket, Rebecca, as it may help you to control your thirst."

Rebecca's heart fluttered. She was to stand in the corner by the water bucket and be stared at by all the students! She moved a step nearer her seat, but was stopped by Miss Dearborn's command in a still firmer voice.

"Stand by the pail, Rebecca! Samuel, how many times have you asked for water today?"

"This is the f-f-fourth."

"Don't touch the dipper, please. The school has done nothing but drink this afternoon; it has had no time to study. I suppose you had something salty for breakfast, Samuel?" asked Miss Dearborn with sarcasm.

"I had salted fish, j-just like Reb-b-becca." (Quiet giggles by the students.)

"I judged so. Stand by the other side of the bucket, Samuel."

Rebecca's head was bowed with shame, and life looked too black a thing to be endured. The punishment was bad enough, but to be coupled in correction with Samuel Simpson was beyond human endurance.

Singing was the last activity of the school day, and Minnie chose "Shall We Gather at the River?" a song that seemed to hold some secret, subtle association with the situation. The students shouted the choral invitation again and again with great energy:

"Shall we gather at the river, the beautiful, the beautiful river?"

Miss Dearborn looked at Rebecca's bent head and saw that the child's face was pale except for two red spots glowing on her cheeks. Tears hung on her lashes, and her breath came and went quickly.

"You may go to your seat, Rebecca," said Miss Dearborn at the end of the first song. "Samuel, stay where you are. Students, I asked Rebecca to stand by the bucket to break up this habit of incessant drinking, which is nothing more than a mindless desire to walk to and fro. Every time Rebecca has asked for a drink today, the whole school has gone to the bucket one after another. She is really thirsty, and I dare say I ought to have punished *you* for following her example, rather than her for setting it. What shall we sing now, Alice?"

"The 'Old Oaken Bucket,' please."

"Think of something dry, Alice, and change the subject. The 'Star-Spangled Banner' if you like or anything else."

Rebecca sank into her seat and pulled the singing book from her desk, Miss Dearborn's public explanation having lifted some of the weight from her heart.

Element Focus: Character

Explain some reasons why you feel Rebecca and Samuel fit well with this setting.

Excerpt from

Treasure Island

by Robert Louis Stevenson

I was standing at the door. I saw someone slowly coming near. He was blind. He tapped before him with a stick. He wore a big green shade over his eyes and nose. He was hunched, as if with age or weakness. He wore a huge old worn sea cloak with a hood. It made him look deformed. I never saw a more awful-looking figure. He stopped a little ways from the inn. He raised his voice in an odd sing-song to address the air in front of him, "Will anyone inform a poor blind man, who lost his precious eyesight in the defense of his beloved England, where or in what part of this country he may be?"

"You are in Black Hill Cove at the Admiral Benbow Inn," I said.

"I hear a young voice," said he. "Will you give me your hand, my young friend, and lead me in?"

I held out my hand. The awful blind man gripped it like a vise. His strength so shocked me that I struggled to pull away. But the blind man pulled me closer with a single pull of his arm.

"Now, boy," he snarled, "take me to the pirate."

"Sir," said I, "I dare not."

He sneered, "Take me in right now, or I will break your arm!" With the threat, he gave my arm such a yank that I cried out.

"Sir," said I, "it is for yourself I worry. The pirate is not who he once was. He sits with a drawn sword. And another man—"

"Come now, march," he interrupted me. I never heard a voice more nasty, cold, and ugly than that blind man's. It scared me more than the pain. I did as he said, walking in the door and towards the parlor. There the sick old pirate was sitting. He was drunk with whiskey. The blind man held me with an iron fist. He leaned almost more of his weight on me than I could stand. "Lead me right up to him, and when I'm in view, cry out, 'Here's a friend for you, Bill,' for if you don't, I will do this." And he gave my arm such a twist that I thought I would faint. I was so afraid of the blind beggar that I forgot my fear of the pirate. I opened the parlor door. I said the words he had told me in a shaking voice.

The old pirate raised his eyes. At one look, the whiskey went out of him. He was left sober. The look on his face was not so much of fear as of deadly illness. He made a move to rise. But he did not have enough strength.

"Now, Bill, sit where you are," said the beggar. "Though I cannot see, I can hear a finger move. Business is business. Hold out your left hand. Boy, take his left hand by the wrist. Bring it to my right."

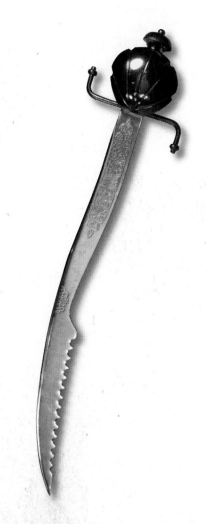

We both did as he said. I saw him pass something from the hollow of the hand that held his stick into the palm of the pirate's, which closed upon it.

"That is done," said the blind man. As he spoke, he let go of me. With amazing accuracy and quickness, he skipped out of the parlor and into the road. I stood still with shock. I heard his stick go tap-tap-tapping into the distance.

Element Focus: Plot

Predict what the blind beggar will be doing next. Explain.

Treasure Island

by Robert Louis Stevenson

I was standing at the door when I saw someone drawing slowly near. He was blind, for he tapped before him with a stick. He wore a big green shade over his eyes and nose. He was hunched, as if with age or weakness. He wore a huge old tattered sea cloak with a hood. It made him look deformed. I never saw a more dreadful-looking figure. He stopped a little ways from the inn. He raised his voice in an odd sing-song to address the air in front of him, "Will anyone inform a poor blind man, who lost his precious eyesight in the defense of his beloved England, where or in what part of this country he may be?"

"You are in Black Hill Cove at the Admiral Benbow Inn," I said.

"I hear a young voice," said he. "Will you give me your hand, my young friend, and lead me in?"

I held out my hand. The horrible, eyeless creature gripped it like a vise. His strength so shocked me that I struggled to pull away, but the blind man pulled me closer with a single action of his arm.

"Now, boy," he snarled, "take me to the pirate."

"Sir," said I, "I dare not."

He sneered, "Take me in immediately, or I'll break your arm!" With the threat, he gave my arm such a wrench that I cried out.

"Sir," said I, "it is for yourself I worry. The pirate is not who he once was. He sits with a drawn sword. And another gentleman—"

"Come now, march," he interrupted me. I never heard a voice more vicious, cold, and hideous than that blind man's. It terrified me more than the pain. I obeyed him at once, walking in the door and towards the parlor. There the sick old pirate was sitting, dazed with whiskey. The blind man held me with an iron fist. He leaned almost more of his weight on me than I could bear. "Lead me straight up to him, and when I'm in view, cry out, 'Here's a friend for you, Bill,' for if you don't, I'll do this." With that he gave my arm such a twist that I thought I would faint. I was so afraid of the blind beggar that I forgot my terror of the pirate. As I opened the parlor door, I said the words he had ordered in a shaking voice.

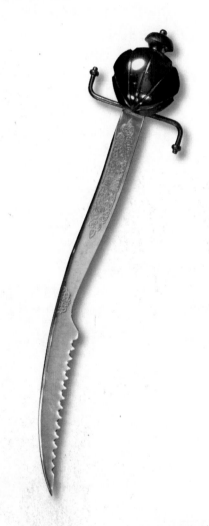

The old pirate raised his eyes. At one look, the whiskey went out of him and left him sober. The look on his face was not so much of terror as of mortal sickness. He made a move to rise, but he did not have enough strength in his body.

"Now, Bill, sit where you are," said the beggar. "Though I can't see, I can hear a finger stirring. Business is business, so hold out your left hand. Boy, take his left hand by the wrist. Bring it near to my right."

We both obeyed him. I saw him pass something from the hollow of the hand that held his walking stick into the palm of the pirate's, which closed upon it.

"That's done," said the blind man. At these words he suddenly let go of me, and with amazing accuracy and nimbleness, skipped out of the parlor and into the road. As I stood still with shock, I could hear his stick go tap-tap-tapping into the distance.

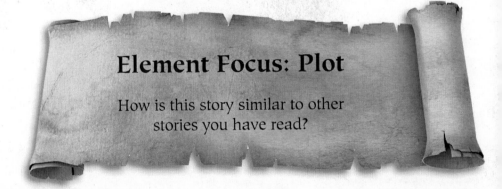

Element Focus: Plot

How is this story similar to other stories you have read?

Excerpt from

Treasure Island

by Robert Louis Stevenson

I was standing at the door when I saw someone drawing slowly near. He was blind, for he tapped before him with a stick and wore a big green shade over his eyes and nose. He was hunched, as if with age or weakness, and wore a huge old tattered sea cloak with a hood that made him look deformed. I never saw a more dreadful-looking figure. He stopped a little ways from the inn and raised his voice in an odd sing-song to address the air in front of him, "Will anyone tell a poor blind man, who has lost the precious sight of his eyes in the defense of his beloved England, where or in what part of this country he may be?"

"You are in Black Hill Cove at the Admiral Benbow Inn," I said.

"I hear a young voice," said he. "Will you give me your hand, my kind young friend, and lead me in?"

I held out my hand. The horrible, eyeless creature gripped it like a vise. His strength so startled me that I struggled to withdraw, but the blind man pulled me closer with a single action of his arm.

"Now, boy," he snarled, "take me to the buccaneer."

"Sir," said I, "I dare not."

He sneered, "Take me in immediately or I'll break your arm!" And with the threat, he gave my arm such a wrench that I cried out.

"Sir," said I, "it is for yourself I worry. The buccaneer is not who he used to be. He sits with a drawn cutlass. And another gentleman—"

"Come now, march," he interrupted, and I never heard a voice more vicious, cold, and hideous than that blind man's. It terrified me more than the pain, and I obeyed him at once, walking straight in the door and towards the parlor. There the sick old buccaneer was sitting, dazed with whiskey. The blind man held me with an iron fist and leaned almost more of his weight on me than I could bear. "Lead me straight up to him, and when I'm in view, cry out, 'Here's a friend for you, Bill,' for if you don't, I'll do this," and with that he gave my arm such a twist that I thought I would faint from pain. I was so completely terrified of the blind beggar that I forgot my terror of the buccaneer. As I opened the parlor door, I cried the words he had ordered in a trembling voice.

The elderly buccaneer raised his eyes, and at one look, the whiskey went out of him and left him sober. The look on his face was not so much of terror as of mortal sickness, and he made a movement to rise, but he had not enough strength in his body.

"Now, Bill, sit where you are," said the beggar. "Though I can't see, I can hear a finger stirring. Business is business, so hold out your left hand. Boy, take his left hand by the wrist. Bring it near to my right."

We both obeyed him. I saw him pass something from the hollow of the hand that held his walking stick into the palm of the buccaneer's, which closed upon it instantly.

"That's done," said the blind man. At these words he suddenly let go of me, and with incredible accuracy and nimbleness, skipped out of the parlor and into the road. As I stood motionless with shock, I could hear his stick go tap-tap-tapping into the distance.

Element Focus: Plot

What is the theme of this story?

Excerpt from

Treasure Island

by Robert Louis Stevenson

I was standing at the door when I saw someone drawing slowly near. He was plainly blind, for he tapped before him with a stick and wore a big green shade over his eyes and nose; and he was hunched, as if with age or weakness, and wore a huge old tattered sea cloak with a hood that made him appear positively deformed. I never saw in my life a more dreadful-looking figure. He stopped a little ways from the inn, and raising his voice in an odd sing-song, addressed the air in front of him, "Will anyone inform a poor blind man, who has lost the precious sight of his eyes in the defense of his beloved England, where or in what part of this country he may now be?"

"You are in Black Hill Cove at the Admiral Benbow Inn," I said.

"I hear a young voice," said he. "Will you give me your hand, my kind young friend, and lead me in?"

I held out my hand, and the horrible, eyeless creature gripped it like a vise. His strength so startled me that I struggled to withdraw, but the blind man pulled me closer with a single action of his arm.

"Now, boy," he snarled, "take me to the buccaneer."

"Sir," said I, "I dare not."

He sneered, "Take me in immediately, or I'll break your arm," and with the threat, he gave my arm such a wrench that I cried out.

"Sir," said I, "it is for yourself I worry. The buccaneer is not who he used to be. He sits with a drawn cutlass, and another gentleman—"

"Come now, march," he interrupted, and I never heard a voice more vicious and cold and hideous than that blind man's. It terrified me more than the pain, and I obeyed him at once, walking straight in the door and towards the parlor, where the sick old buccaneer was sitting, dazed with whiskey. The blind man held me with an iron fist and leaned almost more of his weight on me than I could bear. "Lead me straight up to him, and when I'm in view, cry out, 'Here's a friend for you, Bill,' for if you don't, I'll do this," and with that he gave my arm such a twist that I thought I would faint in agony. I was so utterly terrified of the blind beggar that I forgot my terror of the buccaneer, and as I opened the parlor door, I cried the words he had ordered in a trembling voice.

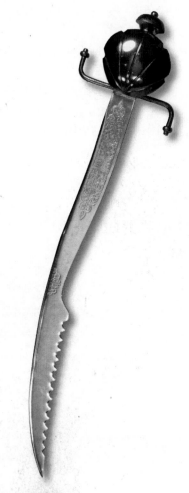

The elderly buccaneer raised his eyes, and at one look, the whiskey went out of him and left him sober. The expression of his face was not so much of terror as of mortal sickness, and he made a movement to rise, but he had not enough strength in his body.

"Now, Bill, sit where you are," said the beggar. "Though I can't see, I can hear a finger stirring. Business is business, so hold out your left hand. Boy, take his left hand by the wrist and bring it near to my right."

We both obeyed him, and I saw him pass something from the hollow of the hand that held his walking stick into the palm of the buccaneer's, which closed upon it instantly.

"That's done," said the blind man, and at these words he suddenly let go of me, and with incredible accuracy and nimbleness, skipped out of the parlor and into the road. As I stood motionless with shock, I could hear his stick go tap-tap-tapping into the distance.

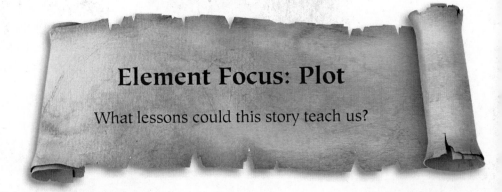

Element Focus: Plot

What lessons could this story teach us?

#50983—Leveled Texts for Classic Fiction: Adventure © Shell Education

Excerpt from

Tarzan of the Apes

by Edgar Rice Burroughs

It was on the morning of the second day that the event occurred. It was the first link in a chain of events. It changed the life for an unborn baby in a way that has never before happened to anyone.

Two men were washing the decks of the *Fuwalda*. The first mate was on duty. The captain stopped to speak with John and Lady Alice. The men were working backwards toward the little group. They were facing away from the sailors. Closer and closer the workers came. At last, one of them was right behind the captain. In another moment he would have passed by. Then this odd tale would not have been written. But just then, the captain turned to leave Lord and Lady Greystoke. As he did, he tripped against the sailor. The captain fell upon the deck. He knocked over the water pail, too. He was drenched in dirty water.

The captain said a string of swear words. His face was red with rage. The captain got to his feet. With a terrific blow, he knocked the sailor to the deck. The man was small and rather old. That made the captain's act even more shocking. The other man was neither old nor small. He was a big bear of a man. He had a black mustache and a thick neck set between huge shoulders. As he saw his mate go down, he crouched. With a snarl, he sprang upon the captain. He struck him a mighty blow. It crushed the captain to his knees.

The captain's face went from red to white. This was mutiny! This captain had stopped mutiny before. Without getting up, he pulled a gun from his pocket. He fired it at the large man standing over him. But, quick as he was, John was almost as quick. The bullet was meant for the sailor's heart. It struck his leg instead. Lord Greystoke had struck the captain's arm when he saw the gun flash in the sun.

Angry words passed between John and the captain. John made it plain that he was upset with the brutality used on the crew. He would not allow anything further of the kind while he and Lady Greystoke were on board. The captain wanted to make an angry reply. But he chose not to. He turned on his heel. He walked away frowning. He did not dare to anger an English official. The English Queen commanded the English navy. He was afraid of her navy.

The two men got up. The older man helped his wounded mate to rise. The big man was Black Michael. He tried to stand on his leg. He found that he could limp on it. He turned to John. He said a gruff word of thanks. His tone was surly. But his words were well meant.

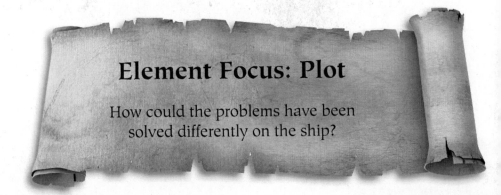

Element Focus: Plot

How could the problems have been solved differently on the ship?

Excerpt from
Tarzan of the Apes

by Edgar Rice Burroughs

It was on the morning of the second day that the first link was formed in a chain of circumstances. It changed the life for one then unborn in a way that has never before happened in the history of man.

Two sailors were washing the decks of the *Fuwalda*. The first mate was on duty. The captain had stopped to speak with John and Lady Alice. The men were working backwards toward the little group. They were facing away from the sailors. Closer and closer the workers came. At last, one of them was right behind the captain. In another moment he would have passed by. Then this strange tale would not have been written. But just that instant, the captain turned to leave Lord and Lady Greystoke. As he did, he tripped against the sailor. The captain sprawled face first upon the deck. He overturned the water pail, too. He was drenched in its dirty contents.

With a string of swear words, his face darkened with the scarlet of rage. The captain got to his feet. With a terrific blow, he knocked the sailor to the deck. The man was small and rather old. That made the brutality of the act even more shocking. The other sailor was neither old nor small. He was a huge bear of a man. He had a fierce black mustache and a great bull neck set between massive shoulders. As he saw his mate go down, he crouched. With a snarl, he sprang upon the captain. He crushed him to his knees with one mighty blow.

The captain's face changed from scarlet to white. This was mutiny! This captain had met and stopped mutiny before in his career. Without rising, he whipped a gun from his pocket. He fired point blank at the great mountain of muscle towering before him. But, quick as he was, John was almost as quick. The bullet meant for the sailor's heart lodged in his leg instead. Lord Greystoke had struck down the captain's arm when he saw the gun flash in the sun.

Angry words passed between John and the captain. John made it plain that he was disgusted with the brutality displayed toward the crew. He would not tolerate anything further of the kind while he and Lady Greystoke were passengers. The captain was on the point of making an angry reply. Thinking better of it, he turned on his heel. Scowling, he strode away. He did not dare to anger an English official. The Queen's mighty arm wielded an instrument which he feared— England's navy.

The two sailors picked themselves up. The older man assisted his wounded mate to rise. The big fellow was known as Black Michael. He tried his leg gingerly. Finding that it bore his weight, he turned to John with a gruff word of thanks. Though the fellow's tone was surly, his words were clearly well meant.

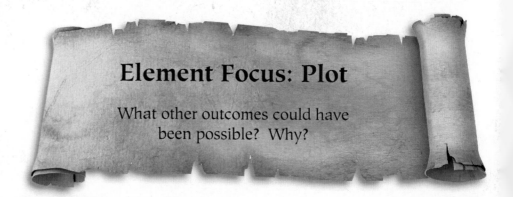

Element Focus: Plot

What other outcomes could have been possible? Why?

Excerpt from
Tarzan of the Apes

by Edgar Rice Burroughs

It was on the morning of the second day that the first link was forged in a chain of circumstances. It changed the life for one then unborn in a way that has never been paralleled in the history of man.

Two sailors were washing down the decks of the *Fuwalda*. The first mate was on duty, and the captain had stopped to speak with John and Lady Alice. The men were working backwards toward the little party. They were facing away from the sailors. Closer and closer they came, until one of them was directly behind the captain. In another moment he would have passed by. Then this strange story would never have been written. But just that instant, the captain turned to leave Lord and Lady Greystoke. As he did so, he tripped against the sailor and sprawled face first upon the deck and overturned the water bucket so that he was drenched in its dirty contents.

With a string of awful oaths, his face suffused with the scarlet of rage, the captain regained his feet. With a terrific blow, he knocked the sailor to the deck. The man was small and rather old. That made the brutality of the act even more shocking. The other sailor was neither old nor small. He was a huge bear of a man with a fierce black mustache and a great bull neck set between massive shoulders. As he saw his mate go down, he crouched. With a low snarl, he sprang upon the captain. He crushed him to his knees with a single mighty blow.

The captain's face changed from scarlet to white, for this was mutiny. This captain had met and subdued mutiny before in his brutal career. Without rising, he whipped a revolver from his pocket. He fired point blank at the great mountain of muscle towering before him. But, quick as he was, John was almost as quick. The bullet intended for the sailor's heart lodged in his leg instead. Lord Greystoke had struck down the captain's arm when he saw the weapon flash in the sun.

Angry words passed between John and the captain. John made it plain that he was disgusted with the brutality displayed toward the crew. He would not tolerate anything further of the kind while he and Lady Greystoke were passengers. The captain was on the point of making an angry reply. Thinking better of it, he turned on his heel. Scowling, he strode aft. He did not dare to anger an English official, for the Queen's mighty arm wielded a punitive instrument which he feared—England's navy.

The two sailors picked themselves up, the older man assisting his wounded mate to rise. The big fellow was known among his mates as Black Michael. He tried his leg gingerly, and, finding that it bore his weight, turned to John with a gruff word of thanks. Though the fellow's tone was surly, his words were clearly well meant.

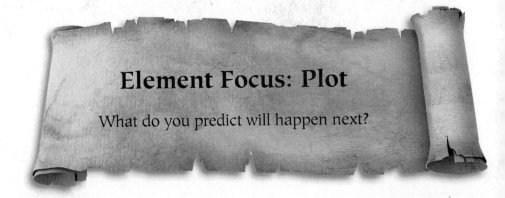

Element Focus: Plot

What do you predict will happen next?

Excerpt from

Tarzan of the Apes

by Edgar Rice Burroughs

It was on the morning of the second day that the first link was forged in a chain of circumstances ending in a life for one then unborn such as has never been paralleled in the history of man.

Two sailors were washing down the decks of the *Fuwalda*. The first mate was on duty, and the captain had stopped to speak with John and Lady Alice. The men were working backwards toward the little party who were facing away from the sailors. Closer and closer they came, until one of them was directly behind the captain. In another moment he would have passed by. Then this strange narrative would never have been written. But just that instant the captain turned to leave Lord and Lady Greystoke. As he did so, he tripped against the sailor and sprawled headlong upon the deck, overturning the water bucket so that he was drenched in its dirty contents.

With a volley of awful oaths, his face suffused with the scarlet of rage, the captain regained his feet. With a terrific blow, he felled the sailor to the deck. The man was small and rather old, so that the brutality of the act was shocking. The other sailor, however, was neither old nor small. He was a huge bear of a man with a fierce black mustache and a great bull neck set between massive shoulders. As he saw his mate go down, he crouched. With a low snarl, he sprang upon the captain, crushing him to his knees with a single mighty blow.

From scarlet the captain's face went white, for this was mutiny. This captain had met and subdued mutiny before in his brutal career. Without waiting to rise, he whipped a revolver from his pocket. He fired point blank at the great mountain of muscle towering before him. But, quick as he was, John was almost as quick, so that the bullet intended for the sailor's heart lodged in the sailor's leg instead. Lord Greystoke had struck down the captain's arm when he saw the weapon flash in the sun.

Bitter words passed between John and the captain. John made it plain that he was disgusted with the brutality displayed toward the crew and he would not tolerate anything further of the kind while he and Lady Greystoke remained passengers. The captain was on the point of making an angry retort, but, thinking better of it, turned on his heel. Scowling, he strode aft. He did not dare to anger an English official, for the Queen's mighty arm wielded a punitive instrument which he feared—England's navy.

The two sailors picked themselves up, the older man assisting his wounded mate to rise. The big fellow was known among his mates as Black Michael. He tried his leg gingerly, and, finding that it bore his weight, turned to John with a gruff word of thanks. Though the fellow's tone was surly, his words were clearly well meant.

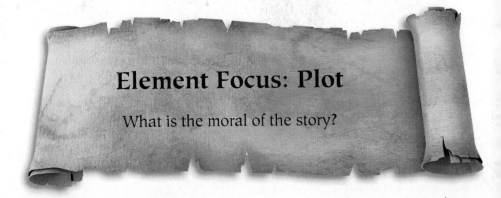

Element Focus: Plot

What is the moral of the story?

The Count of Monte Cristo

by Alexandre Dumas

|||||||||||||||||||||||||||||||||||||||||||||||||||||||||||||||||||||||||||||||||||||||||||||||||||||||||||||||||||||||||||||||||||||

We will leave Danglars feeling his hatred. He wants the ship's owner to think evil of Edmond. Let's follow Edmond Dantes. He enters a small house. It is on the left of the Allees de Meillan. He ran up the dark stairs. He held the railing with one hand. He paused before a half-open door. From it he could see into a small room.

Dantes' father was in the room. The old man did not yet know that the *Pharaon* had arrived in port. He was sitting in a chair. He was arranging the flowers that climbed over the trellis at his window. Just then, he felt an arm thrown around him. A well-known voice behind him cried, "Father—dear father!"

The old man turned around. Seeing his son Edmond, he let out a cry. Then he fell into his arms. He was pale and trembling.

"What is wrong, father? Are you ill?" asked the young man. He was alarmed.

"No, Edmond. No! But I did not expect you. The joy, the shock of seeing you so suddenly—I feel as if I am going to die."

"Come, cheer up, dear father! They say joy never hurts. That is why I came to you without any warning. Come now, smile. Do not look at me so sadly. Here I am back again. We are going to be happy."

"Yes, my boy, so we will," said the old man. "Come tell me all that has happened to you."

"God forgive me," said the young man. "For I am happy, and it comes from the misery of others. Yet I did not seek this good fortune. It just happened. The good Captain Leclere is dead, father. It is probable that, with the aid of Mr. Morrel, I shall take his place. Imagine me a captain at 20! I will have a hundred louis pay. I will share in the profits! Is this not more than a poor sailor like me could have hoped for?"

"Yes," said the old man, "it is very good."

"With the first money I make, I will buy you a small house. It will have a garden in which to plant your flowers. But what is wrong, father? Are you not well?"

"It is nothing," but as he said so, the old man's strength failed him. He fell backwards.

"Father," cried the young man, "a glass of wine will help you. Where do you keep it?"

"No thanks," said the old man. "You need not look for it. I do not want it."

"Father, tell me where it is." Edmond opened two or three cupboards.

"There is no wine," said the old man.

"What, no wine?" cried Edmond Dantes. He looked at the hollow cheeks of the old man. He looked at the empty cupboards. "Have you wanted money, father?"

"I want nothing now that I have you," said the old man.

Element Focus: Plot

Predict what will happen in the story.

Excerpt from

The Count of Monte Cristo

by Alexandre Dumas

We will leave Danglars struggling with his hatred. He wants to make the ship's owner think evil of Edmond. We will follow Edmond Dantes. He enters a small house, on the left of the Allees de Meillan. He ran up four flights of a dark staircase. He held the railing with one hand and paused before a half-open door. From it he could see into a small room.

Dantes' father was in the room. The news of the arrival of the *Pharaon* had not yet reached the old man. He was sitting in a chair, amusing himself by arranging the flowers that climbed over the trellis at his window. Just then, he felt an arm thrown around his body. A well-known voice behind him exclaimed, "Father— dear father!"

The old man turned around. Upon seeing his son Edmond, he uttered a cry and collapsed into his arms, pale and trembling.

"What ails you, dearest father—are you ill?" asked the young sailor, much alarmed.

"No, my dear Edmond—no; but I did not expect you, and the joy, the surprise of seeing you so suddenly—I feel as if I am going to die."

"Come, cheer up, dear father! They say joy never hurts, and thus I came to you without warning. Come now, do smile, instead of looking at me so solemnly. Here I am back from my trip! We are going to be happy."

"Yes, my boy, so we will," replied the old man. "Come and tell me all that has happened to you."

"God forgive me," said the young man, "for rejoicing at happiness caused by another's misery. But I did not seek this event. It has happened, and I cannot pretend to be sorry for it. The good Captain Leclere is dead, father. It is likely that, with the help of Monsieur Morrel, I shall have his position. Imagine me a captain at 20, with a hundred louis pay, plus a share in the profits! Is this not more than a poor sailor like me could have hoped for?"

"Yes," replied the old man, "it is lucky indeed."

"With the first money I make, I will purchase for you a small house with a garden in which to plant your flowers. But what ails you, father—are you unwell?"

"'Tis nothing; it will soon pass away"—but as the old man spoke, his strength failed him. He fell backwards.

"Father," cried the young man. "A glass of wine will help. In which cupboard do you keep your wine?"

"No thanks," replied the old man. "You need not look for it; I do not want it."

"Father, tell me where it is," said Edmond. He opened two or three cupboards.

"There is no wine," the old man admitted.

"What, no wine?" said Edmond Dantes, looking from his father's hollow cheeks to the bare cupboards. "Have you wanted money, father?"

"I want nothing now that I have you," said the old man.

Element Focus: Plot

Propose a solution for Edmond's money problem.

#50983—*Leveled Texts for Classic Fiction: Adventure*   © *Shell Education*

Excerpt from

The Count of Monte Cristo

by Alexandre Dumas

We will leave Danglars struggling with his hatred, and trying to make the shipowner think evil about his comrade. We will follow Edmond Dantes, who entered a small house, on the left of the Allees de Meillan. He rapidly ascended four flights of a dark staircase. He held the baluster with one hand and paused before a half-open door. From it he could see the whole of a small room.

Dantes' father was in the room. The news of the arrival of the *Pharaon* had not yet reached the old man. He was sitting in a chair, amusing himself by arranging the flowers that climbed over the trellis at his window. Suddenly, he felt an arm thrown around his body, and a well-known voice behind him exclaimed, "Father—dear father!"

The old man turned around, and upon seeing his son Edmond, he uttered a cry and collapsed into his arms, pale and trembling.

"What ails you, dearest father—are you ill?" inquired the young sailor, much alarmed.

"No, my dear Edmond—no; but I did not expect you, and the joy, the surprise of seeing you so suddenly—I feel as if I am going to perish."

"Come, cheer up, dear father! They say joy never hurts, and thus I came to you without warning. Come now, do smile, instead of looking at me so solemnly. Here I am back from my voyage, and we are going to be happy."

"Yes, my boy, so we will," responded the old man. "Come and tell me all that has befallen you."

"God forgive me," said the young man, "for rejoicing at happiness derived from another's misery, but I did not seek this fortuitous event; it has happened, and I cannot pretend to lament it. The good Captain Leclere is dead, father, and it is probable that, with the aid of Monsieur Morrel, I shall have his position. Imagine me a captain at 20, with a hundred louis pay, plus a share in the profits! Is this not more than a poor sailor like me could have hoped for?"

"Yes," responded the old man, "it is most fortunate indeed."

"With the first money I make, I will purchase for you a small house with a garden in which to plant clematis, nasturtiums, and honeysuckle. But what ails you, father—are you unwell?"

"'Tis nothing; it will soon pass away"—but as the old man spoke, his strength failed him, and he fell backwards.

"Father," cried the young man, "a glass of wine will revive you. In which cupboard do you keep your wine?"

"No thanks," replied the old man. "You need not look for it; I do not want it."

"Father, tell me where it is," insisted Edmond, and he opened two or three cupboards.

"There is no wine," the old man admitted.

"What, no wine?" said Edmond Dantes, looking from his father's hollow cheeks to the empty cupboards. "Have you wanted money, father?"

"I want nothing now that I have you," said the old man.

Element Focus: Plot

What problems might Edmond's visit with his father create in the future?

Excerpt from

The Count of Monte Cristo

by Alexandre Dumas

We will leave Danglars struggling with the demon of hatred, and endeavoring to insinuate in the ear of the shipowner some evil suspicions against his comrade, and follow Edmond Dantes, who, after having traversed La Canebiere, took the Rue de Noailles, and entering a small house, on the left of the Allees de Meillan, rapidly ascended four flights of a dark staircase, holding the baluster with one hand, while with the other he repressed the beatings of his heart, and paused before a half-open door, from which he could see the whole of a small room.

This room was occupied by Dantes' father. The news of the arrival of the *Pharaon* had not yet reached the old man, who, mounted on a chair, was amusing himself by training with trembling hand the nasturtiums and sprays of clematis that clambered over the trellis at his window. Suddenly, he felt an arm thrown around his body, and a well-known voice behind him exclaimed, "Father—dear father!"

The old man turned around, and, upon seeing his son Edmond, he uttered a cry and collapsed into his arms, pale and trembling.

"What ails you, dearest father—are you ill?" inquired the youthful sailor, much alarmed.

"No, my dear Edmond—no; but I did not expect you, and the joy, the surprise of seeing you so suddenly—I feel as though I am going to perish."

"Come, cheer up, dear father! They say joy never hurts, and thus I came to you without warning. Come now, do smile, instead of looking at me so solemnly. Here I am back from my expedition, and we are going to be happy."

"Yes, my boy, so we will," responded the old man. "Come and explain to me all that has befallen you."

"God forgive me," exclaimed the young man, "for rejoicing at happiness derived from another's misery, but I did not seek this fortuitous event; it has happened, and I cannot pretend to lament it. The good Captain Leclere is dead, father, and it is probable that, with the aid of Monsieur Morrel, I shall have his position. Imagine me a captain at 20, with a hundred louis pay, plus a share in the profits! Is this not more than a penniless sailor like me could have hoped for?"

"Yes," responded the old man, "it is most fortunate indeed."

"With the first money I make, I will purchase for you a small house with a garden in which to plant clematis, nasturtiums, and honeysuckle. But what ails you, father—are you unwell?"

"'Tis nothing; it will soon pass away"—but as the old man spoke, his strength failed him, and he stumbled backwards.

"Father," cried the young man, "a glass of wine will revive you. In which cupboard do you keep your wine?"

"No thanks," replied the old man. "You need not look for it; I do not want it,"

"Father, tell me where it is," insisted Edmond, and he opened two or three cupboards.

"There is no wine," the old man admitted.

"What, no wine?" said Edmond Dantes, looking from his father's hollow cheeks to the empty cupboards. "Have you wanted money, father?"

"I want nothing now that I have you," said the old man.

Element Focus: Plot

How is this story similar to and/or different from other stories you have read?

#50983—*Leveled Texts for Classic Fiction: Adventure*   © *Shell Education*

Excerpt from

The Merry Adventures of Robin Hood

by Howard Pyle

Robin Hood became an outlaw. That is why he went to live in Sherwood Forest. It was his home for many years. Two hundred pounds was the price upon his head. It was a reward. It would be given to the man who would bring him into town.

Robin Hood stayed hidden. He was in the woods for one year. Other men gathered around him. Each had been outlawed. In that year, about a hundred good, strong men joined him. They chose him to be their leader. All of them had been mistreated. Now they swore that they would mistreat those who had wronged them. They would steal from rich men the money that they had taken from the poor. The poor had paid unfair taxes, high land rents, and wrongful fines. Robin and his men would help any poor folk in need or trouble. They would give back to them that which had been taken from them by the rich. The men swore never to harm a child or a woman, too. After a while, the people saw that Robin and his men meant no harm. Instead, poor families were given money or food in time of need. The people praised Robin and his merry men. They told tales of him and his life in Sherwood Forest. They felt him to be one of them.

The Sheriff of Nottingham swore that he himself would get Robin. He wanted the two hundred pounds. The man Robin had killed was the Sheriff's relative. The Sheriff did not know about the men Robin had with him. He wanted to serve a warrant for his arrest. He thought Robin was like any other man who had broken a law. He offered 80 golden angels to any man who would serve the warrant. But the men of Nottingham Town knew more than the Sheriff did. Many laughed to think of handing a warrant to the bold outlaw. They knew that they would get cracked heads if they tried. Two weeks went by. No one came forward. No one would do what the Sheriff wanted. Then he said, "A good reward I offered to anyone would serve a warrant upon Robin Hood. But no one wants to do it."

"Now," thought the Sheriff, "if I could get Robin to come to Nottingham Town, I could grab him. I would lay my hands upon him. He would never get away." Then it came to him like a flash. He would hold a shooting match. He would offer a big prize. Robin Hood might come to the contest. This thought made him say "Aha!" He slapped his palm on his leg.

The Sheriff sent men out. They went north and south. They went east and west. They told about the grand shooting match in each town. Anyone who could draw a longbow could try for the prize. The prize was an arrow of pure gold.

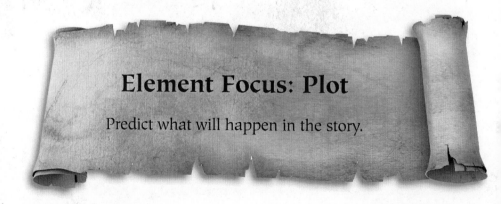

Element Focus: Plot

Predict what will happen in the story.

#50983—Leveled Texts for Classic Fiction: Adventure

Excerpt from

The Merry Adventures of Robin Hood

by Howard Pyle

Robin Hood became an outlaw. That is why he went to live in the forest. It was his home for many years to come. Two hundred pounds were set upon his head. It would be given as a reward to the man who would bring him to justice.

Robin Hood stayed hidden in Sherwood Forest for one year. In that time other men like himself gathered around him. Each had been outlawed for this cause and for that. In that year, a hundred or more good, stout men joined him. They chose him as their leader. They swore that since they had been mistreated, they would mistreat those who had wronged them. They would steal from rich men that which had been taken from the poor by unfair taxes, high land rents, and wrongful fines. They would help any poor folk in need and trouble. They would return to them that which had been taken from them by the rich. The group also swore never to harm a child nor to wrong a woman. After a while, the people saw that Robin and his band meant no harm to them. They saw that money or food came in time of want to many poor families. The people praised Robin and his merry men. They told many tales of him and of his doings in Sherwood Forest. They felt him to be one of them.

The Sheriff of Nottingham swore that he himself would get Robin. He wanted the two hundred pounds. The man Robin had killed was the Sheriff's relative. The Sheriff did not know about the group Robin gathered with him in Sherwood Forest. He thought that he could serve a warrant for his arrest as if he were any other man who had broken a law. He offered 80 golden angels to any man who would serve this warrant. But the men of Nottingham Town knew more than the Sheriff did. Many laughed to think of handing a warrant to the bold outlaw. They knew that all they would get would be cracked heads. Two weeks passed. No one came forward to do the Sheriff's business. Then he said, "A good reward have I offered to whosoever would serve a warrant upon Robin Hood. I wonder why no one wants to do the task."

"Now," thought the Sheriff, "could I but get Robin to come to Nottingham Town, I could grab him. I would lay hands upon him so stoutly that he would never get away." Then it came to him like a flash. He were to hold a shooting match and offer a grand prize, Robin Hood might come to the contest. This thought caused him to cry "Aha!" He slapped his palm upon his thigh.

The Sheriff sent messengers out. They went north and south and east and west. They proclaimed this grand shooting match in every town across the countryside. Anyone was welcome who could draw a longbow. The prize was to be an arrow of pure gold.

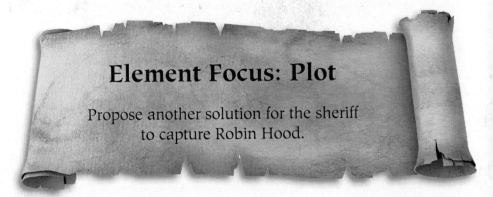

Element Focus: Plot

Propose another solution for the sheriff to capture Robin Hood.

Excerpt from

The Merry Adventures of Robin Hood

by Howard Pyle

Robin Hood became outlawed and that is how he came to dwell in the greenwood. It was to be his home for many a year to come. Two hundred pounds were set upon his head as a reward for whoever would bring him to justice.

Robin Hood stayed hidden in Sherwood Forest for one year. In that time there gathered around him many other men like himself. Each had been outlawed for this cause and for that. In all that year, a hundred or more good, stout men joined him. They chose him to be their leader. Then they vowed that even as they themselves had been mistreated, they would mistreat their oppressors and that

from each they would take that which had been taken from the poor by unfair taxes, high land rents, and wrongful fines. But to the poor folk they would give a helping hand in need and trouble. They would return to them that which had been unfairly taken from them. Besides this, they swore never to harm a child nor to wrong a woman. After a while, when the people saw that no harm was meant to them and that money or food came in time of want to many a poor family, they praised Robin and his merry men. The people told many tales of him and of his doings in Sherwood Forest. They felt him to be one of them.

The Sheriff of Nottingham swore that he himself would seize Robin. He wanted the two hundred pounds. Also, the man Robin had killed was the Sheriff's relative. The Sheriff did not know about the group Robin had about him in Sherwood Forest. He thought that he could serve a warrant for his arrest as if he were any other man who had broken a law. Therefore, he offered 80 golden angels to any man who would serve this warrant. But the men of Nottingham Town knew more of Robin Hood and his doings than the Sheriff did. Many laughed to think of serving a warrant upon the bold outlaw. They knew that all they would get if they tried would be cracked heads. Thus two weeks passed. During that time no one came forward to do the Sheriff's business. Then said he, "A right good reward have I offered to whosoever would serve a warrant upon Robin Hood. I marvel that no one has come to do the task."

"Now," thought the Sheriff, "could I but persuade Robin to come to Nottingham Town, I could find him. I would lay hands upon him so stoutly that he would never get away again." Then it came to him like a flash. He were to proclaim a great shooting match and offer some grand prize, Robin Hood might come to the contest. This thought caused him to cry "Aha!" and slap his palm upon his thigh.

Thus the Sheriff sent messengers north and south and east and west. They proclaimed through every town, hamlet, and across the countryside this grand shooting match. Everyone was welcome who could draw a longbow. The prize was to be an arrow of pure gold.

Element Focus: Plot

What might happen next in this story?

Excerpt from

The Merry Adventures of Robin Hood

by Howard Pyle

Robin Hood became outlawed and that is how he came to dwell in the greenwood that was to be his home for many a year to come. Two hundred pounds were set upon his head as a reward for whoever would dare to bring him to justice.

Robin Hood stayed hidden in Sherwood Forest for one year. In that time there gathered around him many others like himself. Each had been outlawed for this cause and for that, so in all that year, a hundred or more good, stout men joined him, and chose him to be their leader. Then they vowed that even as they themselves had been despoiled, they would despoil their oppressors and that

from each they would take that which had been wrung from the poor by unjust taxes, exorbitant land rents, and wrongful fines. But to the poor folk they would give a helping hand in need and trouble and would return to them that which had been unjustly wrested from them. Besides this, they swore never to harm a child nor to wrong a woman, so that after a while, when the people saw that no harm was meant to them and that money or food came in time of want to many a poor family, they praised Robin and his merry men. The people told many tales of him and of his doings in Sherwood Forest, for they felt him to be one of themselves.

The Sheriff of Nottingham swore that he himself would seize Robin. He wanted the two hundred pounds. Also, the man Robin had killed was the Sheriff's kinsman. The Sheriff did not know what a force Robin had about him in Sherwood Forest. He thought that he could serve a warrant for his arrest just as he could upon any other man who had broken a law. Therefore, he offered 80 golden angels to anyone who would serve this warrant. But the men of Nottingham Town knew more of Robin Hood and his doings than the Sheriff did, and many laughed to think of serving a warrant upon the bold outlaw. They knew that all they would get for such service would be cracked heads. Thus two weeks passed, in which time no one came forward to do the Sheriff's business. Then said he, "A right good reward have I offered to whosoever would serve my warrant upon Robin Hood. I marvel that no one has come to undertake the task."

"Now," thought the Sheriff, "could I but persuade Robin to come to Nottingham Town so that I could find him, I would lay hands upon him so stoutly that he would never get away again." Then it came to him like a flash. Were he to proclaim a great shooting match and offer some grand prize, Robin Hood might attend the contest. This thought caused him to cry "Aha!" and slap his palm upon his thigh.

Thus the Sheriff sent messengers north and south and east and west to proclaim through every town, hamlet, and across the countryside this grand shooting match. Everyone was welcome who could draw a longbow. The prize was to be an arrow of pure gold.

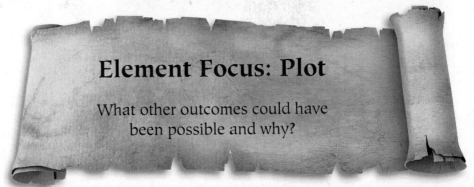

Element Focus: Plot

What other outcomes could have been possible and why?

The Jungle Book

by Rudyard Kipling

||||||||||||||||||||||||||||||||||||||||||||||||||||||||||||||||||||||||||||||||||||||||||||||||||||||||||||||||||

Old books say that when the mongoose fights the snake and gets bitten, he runs off. He eats some herb. It cures him. That is not true. The victory is based on quickness of eye and quickness of foot. It is the snake's blow against the mongoose's jump. As no eye can follow the snake's head as it strikes, this makes things much more wonderful than a magical herb. Rikki-tikki knew he was a young mongoose. It pleased him to think that he had escaped a cobra's strike from behind. It made him proud. When Teddy came running, Rikki-tikki was ready to be petted.

But just as Teddy was stooping, something wriggled in the dust. A tiny voice said, "Be careful. I am Death!" It was Karait. He is the dusty brown snake that lies on the dusty earth. His bite is as deadly as the cobra's. But he is so small that no one thinks of him. So he actually does more harm to people.

Rikki-tikki danced up to Karait with the odd rocking, swaying motion of all the members of his family. It looks funny, but it is a perfectly balanced gait. You can fly off from it at any angle. In dealing with snakes, this is a good thing. Rikki-tikki did not know that he was doing a much more dangerous thing than fighting the cobra. Karait is small and can turn quickly. Unless Rikki bit him close to the back of the head, he would get bitten in his eye or his lip. But Rikki did not know. He rocked back and forth. He looked for a good place to grab hold. Karait struck out. Rikki jumped to the side. Then he tried to run in. But the wicked little dusty gray head lashed within a fraction of his shoulder. Rikki had to jump over the body. The snake's head followed his heels closely.

Teddy shouted to the house, "Oh, look here! Our mongoose is killing a snake." Rikki-tikki heard Teddy's mother scream. His father ran out with a stick. But by the time he came up, Karait had lunged out too far. Rikki-tikki had sprung. He jumped on the snake's back. He dropped his head far between his forelegs. He bit as high up the back as he could get hold. Then he rolled away. That bite paralyzed Karait. Rikki-tikki was about to eat him up from the tail, just as all the members of his family do. Then he remembered that a full meal makes a slow mongoose. If he wanted all his strength and quickness, he must stay thin.

He went away for a dust bath under the bushes. Teddy's father beat the dead Karait.

"What is the use of that?" thought Rikki-tikki. "I have settled it all."

Then Teddy's mother picked him up from the dust. She hugged him. She cried that he had saved Teddy from death.

Element Focus: Language Usage

What pictures do the words paint in your mind?

Excerpt from

The Jungle Book

by Rudyard Kipling

||||||||||||||||||||||||||||||||||||||||||||||||||||||||||||||||||||||||||||||||||||||||||||||||||||||||||||||||||||||||||||||||||||||||||||

Old books say that when the mongoose fights the snake and gets bitten, he runs off. He eats some herb that cures him. That is not true. The victory is based on quickness of eye and quickness of foot—snake's blow against mongoose's jump. As no eye can follow the motion of a snake's head when it strikes, this makes things much more wonderful than any magical herb. Rikki-tikki knew he was a young mongoose. It pleased him to think that he had managed to escape a cobra's strike from behind. It gave him confidence. When Teddy came running down the path, Rikki-tikki was ready to be petted.

But just as Teddy was stooping, something wriggled a little in the dust. A tiny voice said, "Be careful. I am Death!" It was Karait, the dusty brown snake that lies on the dusty earth. His bite is as dangerous as the cobra's. But he is so small that nobody thinks of him. He actually does more harm to people.

Rikki-tikki danced up to Karait with the peculiar rocking, swaying motion that he had inherited from his family. It looks very funny, but it is so perfectly balanced a gait that you can fly off from it at any angle. In dealing with snakes, this is an advantage. If Rikki-tikki had only known, he was doing a much more dangerous thing than fighting the cobra. Karait is small and can turn quickly. Unless Rikki bit him close to the back of the head, he would get the return stroke in his eye or his lip. But Rikki did not know. He rocked back and forth, looking for a good place to grab hold. Karait struck out. Rikki jumped sideways. Then he tried to run in, but the wicked little dusty gray head lashed within a fraction of his shoulder. Rikki had to jump over the body, and the snake's head followed his heels closely.

Teddy shouted to the house, "Oh, look here! Our mongoose is killing a snake." Rikki-tikki heard a scream from Teddy's mother. His father ran out with a stick. But by the time he came up, Karait had lunged out once too far. Rikki-tikki had sprung and jumped on the snake's back. He dropped his head far between his forelegs, bit as high up the back as he could get hold, and rolled away. That bite paralyzed Karait. Rikki-tikki was about to eat him up from the tail, after the custom of his family. Then he remembered that a full meal makes a slow mongoose. If he wanted all his strength and quickness, he must keep himself thin.

He went away for a dust bath under the bushes. Teddy's father beat the dead Karait.

"What is the use of that?" thought Rikki-tikki. "I have settled it all."

Then Teddy's mother picked him up from the dust and hugged him. She cried that he had saved Teddy from death.

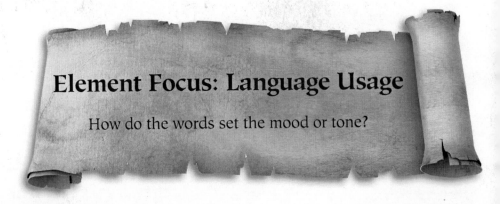

Element Focus: Language Usage

How do the words set the mood or tone?

Excerpt from

The Jungle Book

by Rudyard Kipling

Old books say that when the mongoose fights the snake and gets bitten, he runs off and eats some herb that cures him. That is not true. The victory is only a matter of quickness of eye and quickness of foot—snake's blow against mongoose's jump. As no eye can follow the motion of a snake's head when it strikes, this makes things much more wonderful than any magical herb. Rikki-tikki knew he was a young mongoose, and it pleased him to think that he had managed to escape a cobra's strike from behind. It gave him confidence in himself. When Teddy came running down the path, Rikki-tikki was ready to be petted.

But just as Teddy was stooping, something wriggled a little in the dust, and a tiny voice said, "Be careful. I am Death!" It was Karait, the dusty brown snake that lies on the dusty earth, and his bite is as dangerous as the cobra's. But he is so small that nobody thinks of him, and so he actually does more harm to people.

Rikki-tikki danced up to Karait with the peculiar rocking, swaying motion that he had inherited from his family. It looks very funny, but it is so perfectly balanced a gait that you can fly off from it at any angle. In dealing with snakes, this is an advantage. If Rikki-tikki had only known, he was doing a much more dangerous

thing than fighting the cobra. Karait is so small, and can turn so quickly, that unless Rikki bit him close to the back of the head, he would get the return stroke in his eye or his lip. But Rikki did not know. He rocked back and forth, looking for a good place to grab hold. Karait struck out. Rikki jumped sideways and tried to run in, but the wicked little dusty gray head lashed within a fraction of his shoulder, and he had to jump over the body, and the snake's head followed his heels closely.

Teddy shouted to the house, "Oh, look here! Our mongoose is killing a snake." Rikki-tikki heard a scream from Teddy's mother. His father ran out with a stick, but by the time he came up, Karait had lunged out once too far. Rikki-tikki had sprung, jumped on the snake's back, dropped his head far between his forelegs, bitten as high up the back as he could get hold, and rolled away. That bite paralyzed Karait, and Rikki-tikki was just going to eat him up from the tail, after the custom of his family, when he remembered that a full meal makes a slow mongoose. If he wanted all his strength and quickness ready, he must keep himself thin.

He went away for a dust bath under the bushes, while Teddy's father beat the dead Karait. "What is the use of that?" thought Rikki-tikki. "I have settled it all."

Then Teddy's mother picked him up from the dust and hugged him, crying that he had saved Teddy from death.

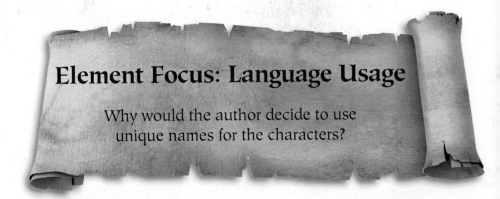

Element Focus: Language Usage

Why would the author decide to use unique names for the characters?

The Jungle Book

by Rudyard Kipling

||||||||||||||||||||||||||||||||||||||||||||||||||||||||||||||||||||||||||||||||||||||||||||||||||||||||||||||||||||||||||

Old books state that when the mongoose fights the snake and gets bitten, he runs off and eats some herb that cures him, which is simply untrue. The victory is only a matter of quickness of eye and quickness of foot—snake's blow against mongoose's jump. Since no eye can follow the motion of a snake's head when it strikes, this makes things much more wonderful than any magical herb. Rikki-tikki knew he was a young mongoose, and it pleased him to think that he had managed to escape a cobra's strike from behind. It gave him such confidence in himself that when Teddy came running down the path, Rikki-tikki was ready to be petted.

But just as Teddy was stooping, something wriggled a little in the dust, and a tiny voice said, "Be careful. I am Death!" It was Karait, the dusty brown snake that lies on the dusty earth, and his bite is as dangerous as the cobra's, but he is so small that nobody thinks of him, and so he actually does the more harm to people.

Rikki-tikki danced up to Karait with the peculiar rocking, swaying motion that he had inherited from his ancestors. It looks very funny, but it is so perfectly balanced a gait that you can fly off from it at any angle. In dealing with snakes, this is an advantage. If Rikki-tikki had only known, he was doing a much more dangerous thing than fighting the cobra. Karait is so small, and can turn so quickly, that unless Rikki bit him close to the back of the head, he would get the return stroke in his eye or his lip. But Rikki did not know this as he rocked back and forth, looking for a good place to grab hold. Karait lashed out. Rikki jumped sideways and tried to run in, but the wicked little dusty gray head lashed within a fraction of his shoulder, and he had to jump over the body, and the snake's head followed his heels closely.

Teddy shouted to the house, "Oh, look here! Our mongoose is killing a snake." Rikki-tikki heard a scream from Teddy's mother. His father rushed out with a stick, but by the time he came up, Karait had lunged out once too far. Rikki-tikki had sprung, jumped on the snake's back, dropped his head far between his forelegs, bitten as high up the back as he could get hold, and rolled away. That bite paralyzed Karait, and Rikki-tikki was just going to eat him up from the tail, after the custom of his family, when he remembered that a full meal makes a slow mongoose. If he wanted all his strength and quickness ready, he must keep himself slender.

He went away for a dust bath under the bushes, while Teddy's father beat the dead Karait. "What is the use of that?" thought Rikki-tikki. "I have settled it all."

Then Teddy's mother picked him up from the dust and hugged him, crying that he had saved Teddy from death.

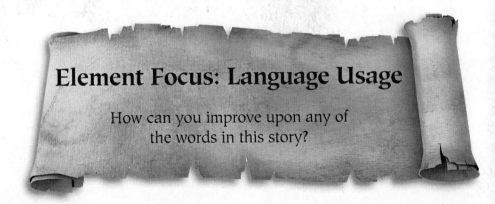

Element Focus: Language Usage

How can you improve upon any of the words in this story?

Excerpt from

What Katy Did

by Susan Coolidge

There were six Carr children. Four were girls. Two were boys. Katy was the oldest. She was twelve years old. Little Phil was the youngest. He was four. The rest fitted in between. Their papa was Dr. Carr. He was a busy man. He was away from home all day. Sometimes he was gone all night, too. He took care of sick people. The children had no mama. She had died when Phil was a baby. That was four years before my story began. Katy could remember her. To the rest she was just a sad, sweet name. Her name was said on Sunday and at prayer-times. Papa spoke of her when he was gentle and solemn.

In place of their mama, there was Aunt Izzie. She was Papa's sister. She came to take care of them when their mama went away on that long journey. For a long time, the little ones kept hoping mama might come back. Aunt Izzie was a small woman. She was sharp-faced and thin. She was rather old-looking, neat, and particular. She meant to be kind to the children. Yet they often puzzled her. They were not like she had been as a child. Aunt Izzie had been a gentle, clean little girl. She loved to sit sewing straight seams. She liked to have her head patted by older people and to be told that she was good. Katy tore her dress every day. She hated sewing. She did not care about being called "good." Clover and Elsie ran off like restless ponies if anyone tried to pat their heads. It was very odd to Aunt Izzie. She found it hard to forgive the children for being so "unaccountable." They were not like the good boys and girls in Sunday-school stories. Those were the young people Aunt Izzie liked. She understood them.

Dr. Carr worried Aunt Izzie, too. He wanted his children to be strong and bold. He liked their climbing and rough play in spite of the bumps and torn clothes it caused. In fact, there was just one half-hour each day when Aunt Izzie felt pleased with the children. That was the half-hour before breakfast. She had made a rule. They were to sit in their chairs and learn a Bible verse. At this time she looked at them with pleased eyes. They were all spick and span. They had nicely brushed jackets and neatly combed hair. But the moment the bell rang, her comfort ended. From then on, the children were what she called "not fit to be seen."

The neighbors felt bad for her. They saw the sixty stiff white pantalette legs hung out to dry each Monday morning. They said to each other what a lot of washing those children made and how hard it must be for poor Miss Carr to keep them so nice. But poor Miss Carr didn't think the children were nice. That was the worst of it. The children minded her pretty well. But they didn't really love her. They called her "Aunt Izzie." She was never "Auntie." Boys and girls will know what that meant.

Element Focus: Language Usage

What is the best description of Aunt Izzie?

#50983—*Leveled Texts for Classic Fiction: Adventure*

Excerpt from

What Katy Did

by Susan Coolidge

There were six Carr children. Four were girls and two were boys. Katy, the oldest, was twelve years old. Little Phil, the youngest, was four. The rest fitted in between. Their papa was Dr. Carr. He was a kind, busy man. He was away from home all day, and sometimes all night, too. He took care of sick people. The children hadn't any mama. She had died when Phil was a baby. That was four years before my story began. Katy could remember her pretty well. To the rest she was but a sad, sweet name. Her name was said on Sunday, and at prayer-times, or when Papa was feeling gentle and solemn.

In place of their mama, whom they remembered dimly, there was Aunt Izzie. She was Papa's sister. She came to take care of them when mama went away on that long journey. For so many months, the little ones kept hoping she might return. Aunt Izzie was a small woman, sharp-faced and thin. She was rather old-looking, very neat, and particular. She meant to be kind to the children. Yet they often puzzled her. They were not a bit like she had been as a child. Aunt

Izzie had been a gentle, tidy little thing. She loved to sit sewing straight seams in the parlor, and to have her head patted by older people, and be told that she was good. Katy tore her dress every day. She hated sewing and didn't care about being called "good." Clover and Elsie shied off like restless ponies if anyone tried to pat their heads. It was very strange to Aunt Izzie. She found it hard to forgive the children for being so "unaccountable." They were so unlike the good boys and girls in Sunday-school stories, who were the young people she liked and understood the most.

 #50983—Leveled Texts for Classic Fiction: Adventure

Dr. Carr also worried Aunt Izzie. He wanted the children to be hardy and bold. He encouraged climbing and rough play, in spite of the bumps and torn clothes which resulted. In fact, there was just one half-hour each day when Aunt Izzie was satisfied about the children. That was the half-hour before breakfast. She had made a rule that they were all to sit in their chairs and learn the Bible verse for the day. At this time she looked at them with pleased eyes. They were all so spick and span, with nicely brushed jackets and neatly combed hair. But the moment the bell rang, her comfort was over. From that time on, the children were what she called "not fit to be seen."

The neighbors pitied her. They used to count the sixty stiff white pantalette legs hung out to dry every Monday morning. They said to each other what a lot of washing those children made and what a chore it must be for poor Miss Carr to keep them so nice. But poor Miss Carr didn't think the children were nice. That was the worst of it. The children minded her pretty well. But they didn't exactly love her. They called her "Aunt Izzie," never "Auntie." Boys and girls will know what that meant.

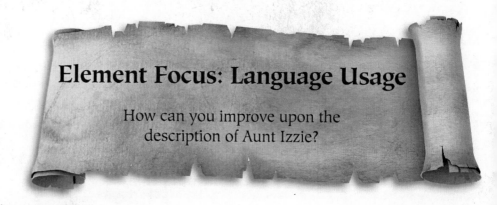

Element Focus: Language Usage

How can you improve upon the description of Aunt Izzie?

What Katy Did

by Susan Coolidge

There were six Carr children. Four were girls and two were boys. Katy, the oldest, was twelve years old. Little Phil, the youngest, was four. The rest fitted in between. Their papa, Dr. Carr, was a kind, busy man. He was away from home all day, and sometimes all night, too, taking care of sick people. The children hadn't any mama. She had died when Phil was a baby, four years before my story began. Katy could remember her pretty well. To the rest she was but a sad, sweet name. Her name was spoken on Sunday, and at prayer-times, or when Papa was especially gentle and solemn.

In place of their mama, whom they remembered so dimly, there was Aunt Izzie. She was Papa's sister. She came to take care of them when mama went away on that long journey, from which, for so many months, the little ones kept hoping she might return. Aunt Izzie was a small woman, sharp-faced and thin, rather old-looking, and very neat and particular. She meant to be kind to the children, but they often puzzled her. They were not a bit like herself when she was a child.

Aunt Izzie had been a gentle, tidy little thing. She loved to sit as Curly Locks did, sewing straight seams in the parlor, and to have her head patted by older people, and be told that she was a good girl. Katy tore her dress every day, hated sewing, and didn't care a button about being called "good." Clover and Elsie shied off like restless ponies when anyone tried to pat their heads. It was very perplexing to Aunt Izzie. She found it hard to quite forgive the children for being so "unaccountable," and so unlike the good boys and girls in Sunday-school memoirs, who were the young people she liked best and understood the most.

Dr. Carr was another person who worried Aunt Izzie. He wished to have the children hardy and bold. He encouraged climbing and rough play, despite the bumps and torn clothes which resulted. In fact, there was just one half-hour of the day when Aunt Izzie was really satisfied about the children, and that was the half-hour before breakfast. She had made a rule that they were all to sit in their chairs and learn the Bible verse for the day. At this time she looked at them with pleased eyes, for they were all so spick and span, with such nicely brushed jackets and such neatly combed hair. But the moment the bell rang, her comfort was over. From that time on, they were what she called "not fit to be seen."

The neighbors pitied her very much. They used to count the sixty stiff white pantalette legs hung out to dry every Monday morning, and say to each other what a lot of washing those children made and what a chore it must be for poor Miss Carr to keep them so nice. But poor Miss Carr didn't think the children were nice. That was the worst of it. The children minded her pretty well, but they didn't exactly love her. They called her "Aunt Izzie," never "Auntie." Boys and girls will know what that meant.

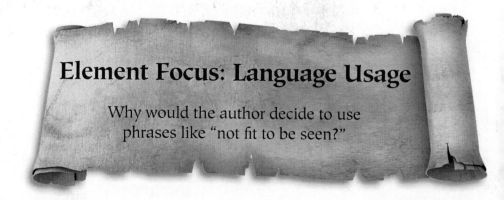

Element Focus: Language Usage

Why would the author decide to use phrases like "not fit to be seen?"

Excerpt from

What Katy Did

by Susan Coolidge

There were six Carr children. Four were girls and two were boys. Katy, the oldest, was twelve years old. Little Phil, the youngest, was four, and the rest fitted in between. Their papa, Dr. Carr, was a kind, busy man, who was away from home all day, and sometimes all night, too, taking care of sick people. The children hadn't any mama. She had died when Phil was a baby, four years before my story began. Katy could remember her pretty well; to the rest she was but a sad, sweet name, spoken on Sunday, and at prayer-times, or when Papa was especially gentle and solemn.

In place of their mama, whom they recollected so dimly, there was Aunt Izzie, Papa's sister. She came to take care of them when mama went away on that long journey, from which, for so many months, the little ones kept hoping she might return. Aunt Izzie was a small woman, sharp-faced and thin, rather old-looking, and very neat and particular about everything. She meant to be kind to the children, but they puzzled her much. They were not a bit like herself when she was a child. Aunt Izzie had been a gentle, tidy little thing, who loved to sit as Curly Locks did, sewing straight seams in the parlor, and to have her head patted by older people, and be told that she was a good girl; whereas Katy tore her dress every day, hated sewing, and didn't care a button about being called "good," and Clover and Elsie shied off like restless ponies when anyone tried to pat their heads. It was very perplexing to Aunt Izzie, and she found it hard to quite forgive the children for being so "unaccountable," and so unlike the good boys and girls in Sunday-school memoirs, who were the young people she liked best and understood the most.

Dr. Carr was another person who worried Aunt Izzie. He wished to have the children hardy and bold and encouraged climbing and rough play, despite the bumps and ragged clothes which resulted. In fact, there was just one half-hour of the day when Aunt Izzie was really satisfied about her charges, and that was the half-hour before breakfast, when she had made a rule that they were all to sit in their chairs and learn the Bible verse for the day. At this time she looked at them with pleased eyes, for they were all so spick and span, with such nicely brushed jackets and such neatly combed hair. But the moment the bell rang, her comfort was over. From that time on, they were what she called "not fit to be seen."

The neighbors pitied her very much. They used to count the sixty stiff white pantalette legs hung out to dry every Monday morning, and say to each other what a lot of washing those children made, and what a chore it must be for poor Miss Carr to keep them so nice. But poor Miss Carr didn't think the children were at all nice—that was the worst of it. The children minded her pretty well, but they didn't exactly love her. They called her "Aunt Izzie," never "Auntie." Boys and girls will know what that meant.

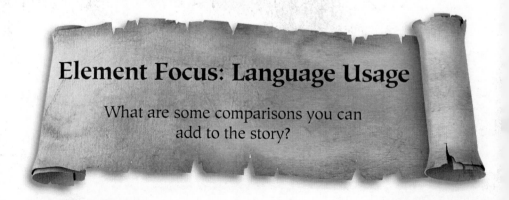

Element Focus: Language Usage

What are some comparisons you can add to the story?

Excerpt from

Call of the Wild

by Jack London

Buck did not read the paper. If he had, he would have known that trouble was coming. All dogs on the West Coast, strong of muscle and with warm hair, were in danger. Men had found gold in the Arctic. When ships told of the find, thousands of men rushed North. These men wanted dogs. The dogs they wanted were heavy, with strong muscles and thick fur coats.

Buck lived at a big house. It was in the sunny Santa Clara Valley. Judge Miller's place stood back from the road. It was half hidden among trees. Through the trees, glances could be caught of the wide porch. It ran around on four sides. A driveway led to the house. It wound through a wide lawn and under the branches of tall trees. Things were even more spread out in the back. In the big stables, a dozen grooms and boys worked. There were rows of vine-covered cabins. There were grape arbors and green fields. There were orchards and berry patches. There was a well pump and a big swimming tank. There, Judge Miller's boys took a morning dip and kept cool in the afternoons.

Over this whole place Buck ruled. Here he was born. Here he had lived the four years of his life. There were other dogs. There had to be other dogs on such a big place. But those dogs did not count. They came and went. They lived in the kennels or in the house. There was Toots. He was a Japanese chin. There was Ysabel. She was a Mexican hairless. These house dogs rarely put nose outdoors or set foot to ground. There were twenty fox terriers, too. They yelped threats at the house dogs, who looked out of the windows.

Buck was neither a house dog nor a kennel dog. The whole place was his. He jumped into the swimming tank with the Judge's sons. He went hunting with them. He went with the Judge's daughters on long walks. On cold nights, he lay at the Judge's feet in front of a warm fire. He carried the Judge's grandsons on his back. He rolled them in the grass. He watched over their adventures in the stable and the berry patches. Among the terriers he walked like royalty. Toots and Ysabel he ignored. He was king over all things of Judge Miller's place. That included the people.

His father was a huge St. Bernard. He had been the Judge's favorite dog. Buck meant to follow in his father's place. He was not as big. He weighed just 140 pounds. His mother had been a Scotch shepherd dog. Even so, 140 pounds, plus the dignity that comes of respect, let Buck carry himself in a regal manner. In the years since his birth, he had developed a pride that was a bit selfish, as men sometimes are. Hunting and running had kept him lean and hardened his muscles. He loved to swim. This was Buck in the fall of 1897. That was when the Klondike strike drew men into the frozen North.

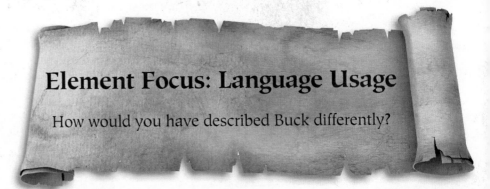

Element Focus: Language Usage

How would you have described Buck differently?

Excerpt from

Call of the Wild

by Jack London

Buck did not read the newspaper. If he had, he would have known that trouble was brewing. Every dog, strong of muscle and with warm hair, from Puget Sound to San Diego, was in danger. Men had found a yellow metal in the Arctic. When steamships told of the find, thousands of men rushed North. These men wanted dogs. The dogs they wanted were heavy, with strong muscles for toil and thick fur coats to keep them from the cold.

Buck lived at a big house in the sunny Santa Clara Valley. It was Judge Miller's place. It stood back from the road, half hidden among trees. Through the trees, glimpses could be caught of the wide porch. It ran around its four sides. The house was reached by a driveway. It wound through a wide lawn and under the boughs of tall trees. Things were even more spacious in the rear. In the large stables, a dozen grooms and boys worked. There were rows of vine-covered servants' cottages. There were long grape arbors and green fields. There were orchards and berry patches. There was a well pump and a big cement swimming tank. There Judge Miller's boys took their morning plunge and kept cool in the afternoons.

Over this whole domain Buck ruled. Here he was born. Here he had lived the four years of his life. There were other dogs. There could not help but be other dogs on so vast a place. But those dogs did not count. They came and went. They lived in the kennels or in the house. There was Toots, the Japanese chin, and Ysabel, the Mexican hairless. These odd creatures rarely put nose outdoors or set foot to ground. On the other hand, there were the fox terriers, twenty of them. They yelped fearful threats at Toots and Ysabel, who looked out of the windows.

Buck was neither a house dog nor a kennel dog. The whole realm was his. He plunged into the swimming tank or went hunting with the Judge's sons. He went with Molly and Alice, the Judge's daughters, on long walks. On cold nights, he lay at the Judge's feet before the roaring fire. He carried the Judge's grandsons on his back or rolled them in the grass. He guarded them in their adventures down to the stable and the berry patches. Among the terriers he walked like royalty. Toots and Ysabel he ignored. He was king over all things of Judge Miller's place, humans included.

His father, Elmo, was a huge St. Bernard. He had been the Judge's favorite companion. Buck meant to follow in his father's place. He was not as large; he weighed just 140 pounds. His mother had been a Scotch shepherd dog. Even so, 140 pounds, to which was added the dignity that comes of universal respect, let him carry himself in a regal manner. During the years since his birth, he had developed a pride that was a bit selfish, like country gentlemen sometimes are. Hunting and running had kept down the fat and hardened his muscles. He loved to swim. This was Buck in the fall of 1897, when the Klondike strike drew men from all the world into the frozen North.

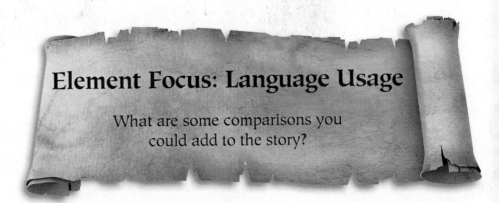

Element Focus: Language Usage

What are some comparisons you could add to the story?

Excerpt from

Call of the Wild

by Jack London

Buck did not read the newspapers, or he would have known that trouble was brewing. Every dog, strong of muscle and with warm hair, from Puget Sound to San Diego was in danger. Men groping in the Arctic darkness had found a yellow metal. When steamship companies had boasted the find, thousands of men rushed North. These men wanted dogs—heavy dogs, with strong muscles by which to toil and thick fur coats to protect them from the bitter cold.

Buck lived at a big house in the sun-kissed Santa Clara Valley. It was called Judge Miller's place. It stood back from the road, half hidden among the trees. Through the trees, glimpses could be caught of the wide porch that ran around its four sides. The house was reached by a driveway which wound through a wide-spreading lawn and under the boughs of tall poplars. Things were even more spacious in the rear. There were large stables, where a dozen grooms and boys worked, rows of vine-covered servants' cottages, long grape arbors, green pastures, orchards, and berry patches. There was the pump for the well, and a big cement swimming tank. There Judge Miller's boys took their morning plunge and kept cool in the hot afternoons.

Over this whole domain Buck ruled. Here he was born, and here he had lived the four years of his life. There were other dogs. There could not help but be other dogs on so vast a place. But they did not count. They came and went, resided in the kennels, or lived in the house. There was Toots, the Japanese chin, and Ysabel, the Mexican hairless. These strange creatures rarely put nose out of doors or set foot to ground. On the other hand, there were the fox terriers, twenty of them. They yelped fearful threats at Toots and Ysabel, who looked out of the windows.

Buck was neither a house dog nor a kennel dog. The whole realm was his. He plunged into the swimming tank or went hunting with the Judge's sons. He escorted Molly and Alice, the Judge's daughters, on their twilight or early morning walks. On wintry nights he lay at the Judge's feet before the roaring fire. He carried the Judge's grandsons on his back or rolled them in the grass. He guarded them in their wild adventures down to the stable yard and the berry patches. Among the terriers he stalked like royalty. Toots and Ysabel he ignored. He was king over all things of Judge Miller's place, humans included.

His father was Elmo, a huge St. Bernard. He had been the Judge's favorite companion, and Buck meant to follow in his father's footsteps. He was not as large; he weighed only 140 pounds. His mother had been a Scotch shepherd dog. Nevertheless, 140 pounds, to which was added the dignity that comes of universal respect, allowed him to carry himself in a regal manner. During the years since his birth, he had developed a pride in himself that was a bit egotistical, as country gentlemen sometimes are. Hunting and running had kept down the fat and hardened his muscles, and he loved to swim. This was Buck in the fall of 1897, when the Klondike strike pulled men from all the world into the frozen North.

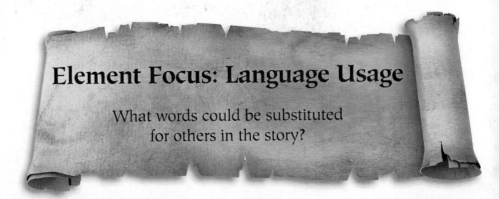

Element Focus: Language Usage

What words could be substituted
for others in the story?

#50983—*Leveled Texts for Classic Fiction: Adventure* © *Shell Education*

Excerpt from

Call of the Wild

by Jack London

Buck did not read the newspapers, or he would have known that trouble was brewing. It was not just for himself, but for every dog, strong of muscle and with warm hair, from Puget Sound to San Diego. Men groping in the Arctic darkness had found a yellow metal. When steamship companies had boasted the find, thousands of men went rushing North. These men wanted dogs—heavy dogs, with strong muscles by which to toil and thick fur coats to protect them from the bitter cold.

Buck lived at a big house in the sun-kissed Santa Clara Valley called Judge Miller's place. It stood back from the road, half hidden among the trees, through which glimpses could be caught of the wide porch that ran around its four sides. The house was approached by a driveway which wound through a wide-spreading lawn and under the boughs of tall poplars. Things were even more spacious in the rear. There were large stables, where a dozen grooms and boys worked, rows of vine-covered servants' cottages, long grape arbors, green pastures, orchards, and berry patches. There was the pump for the well, and a big cement swimming tank where Judge Miller's boys took their morning plunge and kept cool in the hot afternoons.

Over this whole domain Buck ruled. Here he was born, and here he had lived the four years of his life. There were other dogs—there could not help but be other dogs on so vast a place—but they did not count. They came and went, resided in the kennels, or lived in the house. There was Toots, the Japanese chin, and Ysabel, the Mexican hairless,—strange creatures that rarely put nose out of doors or set foot to ground. On the other hand, there were the fox terriers—twenty of them. They yelped fearful threats at Toots and Ysabel, who looked out of the windows.

Buck was neither a house dog nor a kennel dog. The whole realm was his. He plunged into the swimming tank or went hunting with the Judge's sons. He escorted Molly and Alice, the Judge's daughters, on long twilight or early morning walks. On wintry nights he lay at the Judge's feet before the roaring fire. He carried the Judge's grandsons on his back, or rolled them in the grass, and guarded their footsteps on their wild adventures down to the stable yard and the berry patches. Among the terriers he stalked imperiously. Toots and Ysabel he ignored, for he was king over all things of Judge Miller's place, humans included.

His father, Elmo, a huge St. Bernard, had been the Judge's favorite companion, and Buck meant to follow in his father's footsteps. He was not as large—he weighed only 140 pounds—for his mother had been a Scotch shepherd dog. Nevertheless, 140 pounds, to which was added the dignity that comes of universal respect, enabled him to carry himself in a regal manner. During the four years since his birth, he had developed a pride in himself and was even a bit egotistical, as country gentlemen sometimes become. Hunting and running had kept down the fat and hardened his muscles, and he loved to swim. This was Buck in the fall of 1897, when the Klondike strike pulled men from all the world into the frozen North.

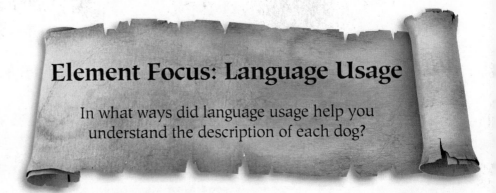

Element Focus: Language Usage

In what ways did language usage help you understand the description of each dog?

#50983—*Leveled Texts for Classic Fiction: Adventure*

Kidnapped

by Robert Louis Stevenson

I asked my uncle if he and my father had been twins.

He jumped upon his stool. The spoon fell out of his hand. It hit the floor. "What makes ye ask that?" he said. He caught me by the front of my coat. This time he looked right into my eyes. His own eyes were little, light, and bright like a bird's. He was blinking and winking oddly.

"What do you mean?" I asked, calmly. I was stronger than he, and not easily scared. "Take your hand from my coat! This is no way to act."

My uncle made an effort to calm himself. "Davie," he said, "ye should not speak to me about your father. That is a mistake." He sat awhile and shook. He kept blinking. "He was the only brother I had," he added. But there was no heart in his voice. Then he took up his spoon. He went on eating. He was still shaking.

Now this last bit, this grabbing me and suddenly stating love for my dead father, was so shocking that it gave me both fear and hope. On the one hand, I began to think my uncle was crazy. He might even be dangerous. On the other hand, there came into my mind a story or some song I had heard. It told of a poor lad. He was a rightful heir and a wicked relative tried to keep him from it. After all, why should my uncle play a part with a relative that came to him without a cent—unless he had a reason to fear him?

With this idea in mind, I began to copy his secret glances. We sat at the table like a cat and a mouse. Each was secretly eyeing the other. He did not say another word. He was turning something over in his mind. The longer we sat and the more I looked at him, the more sure I was that that something was not friendly to me.

When he had cleared the plate, he got out a pipe. He filled it with tobacco. Then he turned around a stool into the corner. He sat awhile smoking. He kept his back to me.

"Davie," he said, at length, "I have been thinking." Then he paused. He went on. "There is a wee bit that I promised ye before ye were born," he said. "I promised it to your father. Oh, nothing legal, ye know. I kept a bit of money aside. It was a great expense. But a promise is a promise. Now it has grown to be just exactly"—and he paused and stumbled— "just exactly 40 pounds!" This last he spoke with a glance over his shoulder. Then he added, almost in a scream, "Scots!"

The pound Scots was the same thing as an English shilling. The difference made by this second statement was large. I could see that the whole story was a lie. It had been invented for some reason. I was puzzled.

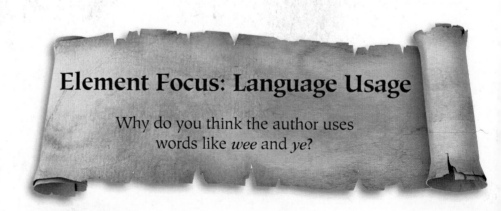

Element Focus: Language Usage

Why do you think the author uses words like *wee* and *ye*?

#50983—Leveled Texts for Classic Fiction: Adventure

© Shell Education

Excerpt from

Kidnapped

by Robert Louis Stevenson

I asked my uncle if he and my father had been twins.

He jumped upon his stool. The spoon fell out of his hand. It hit the floor. "What makes ye ask that?" he said. He caught me by the breast of the jacket. This time he looked straight into my eyes. His own were little, light, and bright like a bird's. He was blinking and winking strangely.

"What do you mean?" I asked, calmly. I was far stronger than he, and not easily frightened. "Take your hand from my jacket! This is no way to behave."

My uncle made a great effort to control himself. "Davie," he said, "ye should not speak to me about your father. That is a mistake." He sat awhile and shook, blinking. "He was all the brother that I ever had," he added. But there was no heart in his voice. Then he caught up his spoon and fell to supper again. He was still shaking.

Now this last bit, this grabbing me and suddenly professing love for my dead father, was so incredible that it filled me with both fear and hope. On the one hand, I began to think my uncle was perhaps insane. He might even be dangerous. On the other hand, there came into my mind a story or some ballad I had heard. It was of a poor lad that was a rightful heir and a wicked relative that tried to keep him from it. After all, why should my uncle play a part with a relative that came to him almost a beggar—unless he had some reason to fear him?

With this idea getting firmly settled in my head, I now began to copy his secret glances. We sat at the table like a cat and a mouse. Each was secretly eyeing the other. Not another word did he say to me. He was busy turning something secretly over in his mind. The longer we sat and the more I looked at him, the more certain I was that that something was not friendly to me.

When he had cleared his plate, he got out a pipeful of tobacco. He turned around a stool into the chimney corner. He sat awhile smoking. He kept his back to me.

"Davie," he said, at length, "I've been thinking." Then he paused and went on. "There's a wee bit that I half promised ye before ye were born," he said. "I promised it to your father. Oh, nothing legal, ye know. Well, I kept a bit of money aside—it was a great expense. But a promise is a promise. Now it has grown to be just exactly"— and here he paused and stumbled— "just exactly 40 pounds!" This last he spoke with a glance over his shoulder. The next moment he added, almost in a scream, "Scots!"

The pound Scots was the same thing as an English shilling. The difference made by this second statement was large. I could see, besides, that the whole story was a lie. It had been invented for some reason which it puzzled me to guess.

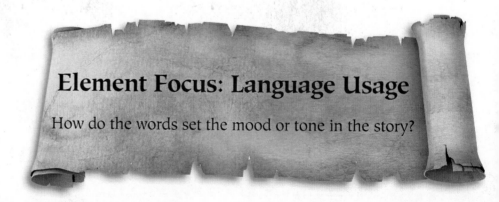

Element Focus: Language Usage

How do the words set the mood or tone in the story?

#50983—Leveled Texts for Classic Fiction: Adventure

Kidnapped

by Robert Louis Stevenson

||||||||||||||||||||||||||||||||||||||||||||||||||||||||||||||||||||||||||||||||||||||||||||||||||||||||||||||||||||||||||||||||||

I asked my uncle if he and my father had been twins.

He jumped upon his stool. The spoon fell out of his hand upon the floor. "What gars ye ask that?" he said. He caught me by the breast of the jacket, and looked this time straight into my eyes. His own were little and light and bright like a bird's, blinking and winking strangely.

"What do you mean?" I asked, very calmly, for I was far stronger than he, and not easily frightened. "Take your hand from my jacket; this is no way to behave."

My uncle made a great effort to control himself. "Davie," he said, "ye should-nae speak to me about your father. That's where the mistake is." He sat awhile and shook, blinking. "He was all the brother that I ever had," he added, but there was no heart in his voice. Then he caught up his spoon and fell to supper again, but still shaking.

Now this last passage, this laying of hands upon me and sudden profession of love for my dead father, was so far beyond my understanding that it left me with both fear and hope. On the one hand, I began to think my uncle was perhaps insane and might be dangerous. On the other hand, there came into my mind (quite unbidden by me and even discouraged) a story or some ballad I had heard folk singing. It was of a poor lad that was a rightful heir and a wicked relative that tried to keep him from it. After all, why should my uncle play a part with a relative that came to him almost a beggar—unless he had some reason to fear him?

With this idea getting firmly settled in my head, I now began to imitate his covert looks. We sat at the table like a cat and a mouse, each secretly observing the other. Not another word did he say to me, black or white. He was busy turning something secretly over in his mind. The longer we sat and the more I looked at him, the more certain I was that that something was not friendly to me.

When he had cleared the plate, he got out a pipeful of tobacco, just as in the morning. He turned around a stool into the chimney corner, and sat awhile smoking. He kept his back to me.

"Davie," he said, at length, "I've been thinking." Then he paused and went on. "There's a wee bit that I half promised ye before ye were born," he continued. "I promised it to your father. O, naething legal, ye understand. Well, I keepit that bit money separate—it was a great expense, but a promise is a promise. Now it has grown to be just precisely— just exactly"—and here he paused and stumbled—"just exactly 40 pounds!" This last he spoke with a sidelong glance over his shoulder. The next moment he added, almost in a scream, "Scots!"

The pound Scots being the same thing as an English shilling, the difference made by this second statement was large. I could see, besides, that the whole story was a lie, invented with some end which it puzzled me to guess.

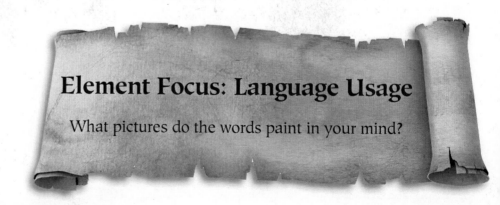

Element Focus: Language Usage

What pictures do the words paint in your mind?

Kidnapped

by Robert Louis Stevenson

I asked my uncle if he and my father had been twins.

He jumped upon his stool, and the spoon fell out of his hand upon the floor. "What gars ye ask that?" he said, and he caught me by the breast of the jacket, and looked this time straight into my eyes: his own were little and light and bright like a bird's, blinking and winking strangely.

"What do you mean?" I asked, very calmly, for I was far stronger than he, and not easily frightened. "Take your hand from my jacket; this is no way to behave."

My uncle seemed to make a great effort to control himself. "Davie," he said, "ye should-nae speak to me about your father. That's where the mistake is." He sat awhile and shook, blinking in his plate: "He was all the brother that ever I had," he added, but with no heart in his voice; and then he caught up his spoon and fell to supper again, but still shaking.

Now this last passage, this laying of hands upon my person and sudden profession of love for my dead father, went so far beyond my comprehension that it put me into both fear and hope. On the one hand, I began to think my uncle was perhaps insane and might be dangerous; on the other, there came up into my mind (quite unbidden by me and even discouraged) a story or some ballad I had heard folk singing of a poor lad that was a rightful heir and a wicked kinsman that tried to keep him from his own. For why should my uncle play a part with a relative that came almost a beggar to his door unless in his heart he had some cause to fear him?

With this notion getting firmly settled in my head, I now began to imitate his covert looks; so that we sat at the table like a cat and a mouse, each stealthily observing the other. Not another word had he to say to me, black or white, but was busy turning something secretly over in his mind; and the longer we sat and the more I looked at him, the more certain I became that that something was unfriendly to myself.

When he had cleared the platter, he got out a single pipeful of tobacco, just as in the morning, turned round a stool into the chimney corner, and sat awhile smoking, with his back to me.

"Davie," he said, at length, "I've been thinking"; then he paused and went on. "There's a wee bit that I half promised ye before ye were born," he continued; "promised it to your father. O, naething legal, ye understand. Well, I keepit that bit money separate—it was a great expense, but a promise is a promise—and it has grown by now to be a matter of just precisely—just exactly"—and here he paused and stumbled— "just exactly 40 pounds!" This last he spoke with a sidelong glance over his shoulder; and the next moment he added, almost in a scream, "Scots!"

The pound Scots being the same thing as an English shilling, the difference made by this second statement was considerable; I could see, besides, that the whole story was a lie, invented with some end which it puzzled me to guess.

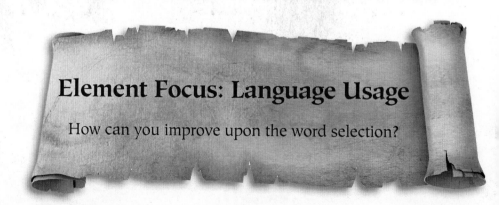

Element Focus: Language Usage

How can you improve upon the word selection?

References Cited

Bean, Thomas. 2000. Reading in the Content Areas: Social Constructivist Dimensions. In *Handbook of Reading Research, vol. 3*, eds. M. Kamil, P. Mosenthal, P. D. Pearson, and R. Barr. Mahwah, NJ: Lawrence Erlbaum.

Bromley, Karen. 2004. Rethinking Vocabulary Instruction. *The Language and Literacy Spectrum* 14:3–12.

Melville, Herman. 1851. *Moby Dick*. New York: Harper.

Nagy, William, and Richard C. Anderson. 1984. How Many Words Are There in Printed School English? *Reading Research Quarterly* 19 (3): 304–330.

National Governors Association Center for Best Practices and Council of Chief State School Officers. 2010. Common Core Standards. http://www.corestandards.org/the-standards.

Oatley, Keith. 2009. Changing Our Minds. *Greater Good: The Science of a Meaningful Life*, Winter. http://greatergood.berkeley.edu/article/item/chaning_our_minds.

Pinnell, Gay Su. 1988. Success of Children At Risk in a Program that Combines Writing and Reading. *Technical Report No.* 417 (January). Reading and Writing Connections.

Richek, Margaret. 2005. Words Are Wonderful: Interactive, Time-Efficient Strategies to Teach Meaning Vocabulary. *The Reading Teacher* 58 (5): 414–423.

Riordan, Rick. 2005. *The Lightning Thief*. London: Puffin Books.

Sachar, Louis. 2000. *Holes*. New York, NY: Dell Yearling.

Snicket, Lemony. 1999. *A Series of Unfortunate Events*. New York: HarperCollins.

Tomlinson, Carol Ann and Marcia. B. Imbeau. 2010. *Leading and Managing a Differentiated Classroom*. Alexandria, VA: Association for Supervision and Curriculum Development.

Zunshine, Lisa. 2006. *Why We Read Fiction: Theory of Mind and the Novel*. Columbus, OH: The Ohio State University Press.

Contents of the Digital Resource CD

Passage	Filename	Pages
Robinson Crusoe	robinson.pdf robinson.doc	31–38
Hans Brinker	hansbrinker.pdf hansbrinker.doc	39–46
The Adventures of Tom Sawyer	tomsawyer.pdf tomsawyer.doc	47–54
The Swiss Family Robinson	swissfamily.pdf swissfamily.doc	55–62
The Adventures of Huckleberry Finn	huckleberry.pdf huckleberry.doc	63–70
The Railway Children	railwaychildren.pdf railwaychildren.doc	71–78
Rebecca of Sunnybrook Farm	rebecca.pdf rebecca.doc	79–86
Treasure Island	treasure.pdf treasure.doc	87–94
Tarzan of the Apes	tarzanapes.pdf tarzanapes.doc	95–102
The Count of Monte Cristo	montecristo.pdf montecristo.doc	103–110
The Merry Adventures of Robin Hood	robinhood.pdf robinhood.doc	111–118
The Jungle Book	junglebook.pdf junglebook.doc	119–126
What Katy Did	katydid.pdf katydid.doc	127–134
Call of the Wild	callofwild.pdf callofwild.doc	135–142
Kidnapped	kidnapped.pdf kidnapped.doc	143–150